Krasna touched the board. A small dot of light appeared in the heart of the tank and went out again. At the same time, there was a small *beep* of sound. Then the tape began to unroll and a scene developed within the cube. The set seemed to be an office much like this one, though that had now gone quite dark; but the clothing was definitely period.

'As you suspected,' Krasna's voice said conversationally in the dimness, over the rising voices of the actors, 'the Service is infallible—within limits. How it got to be that way is a story that started several centuries back.'

Also in Arrow by James Blish

Jack of Eagles
Midsummer Century
The Seedling Stars
A Case of Conscience

CITIES IN FLIGHT SERIES

They Shall Have Stars
A Life for the Stars
Earthman, Come Home
A Clash of Cymbals

James Blish

THE QUINCUNX OF TIME

ARROW BOOKS

Arrow Books Ltd
3 Fitzroy Square, London W1

An imprint of the Hutchinson Publishing Group

London Melbourne Sydney Auckland
Wellington Johannesburg and agencies
throughout the world

First published in Great Britain by Faber and Faber Ltd 1975
Arrow edition 1976
© 1957, 1973, 1975 by James Blish

CONDITIONS OF SALE: This book shall not, by
way of trade or otherwise, be lent, re-sold, hired
out or otherwise circulated without the publisher's
prior consent in any form of binding or cover
other than that in which it is published and
without a similar condition being imposed on
the subsequent purchaser. This book is published
at a net price and is supplied subject to the Publishers Association Standard Conditions of Sale
registered under the Restrictive Trade Practices
Act, 1956.

Made and printed in Great Britain
by The Anchor Press Ltd
Tiptree, Essex

ISBN 0 09 913220 6

to
PAUL SHACKLEY
who reads my stories
far more closely than
I (sometimes) think
they deserve

CONTENTS

A CRITICAL PREFACE: *To Be Skipped by Friends of Fiction*

As is honestly shown a few pages earlier, along with the copyright notice and other matters which publishers call "indicia," this book began life as a short story of some 14,000 words, first published in a magazine in 1954. Even then it was not much of a story by ordinary narrative standards. When William Sloane anthologized it the same year (in *Stories for Tomorrow*, Funk and Wagnalls), he said in his introduction, with almost excessive kindness, that the yarn was "not redundant with physical action" and that in fact it had only a "slight pattern of outward events." These strictures were quite true, and hence I was all the more astonished when André Norton subsequently included the piece in an anthology for teenage readers called *Space Police* (World, 1956). Miss Norton did cut out of it some of the references to drinking, but she left intact all of what Mr. Sloane thought would jolt or numb even new adult readers—the hard stuff about physics and philosophy.

Padding a short story out into a novel is not ordinarily regarded as good practice, either, and since I have been accused a few times by some putative friends of doing exactly this, I was further startled to be asked by editor Larry Shaw to do it to that unpromising, almost plotless story called "Beep." On the other hand, Mr. Shaw had been the first to see some sense and merit in a novella of mine which eventually became a very successful novel called *A Case of Conscience* (1958), so I felt obligated to take a second look.

9

I made two interesting discoveries. The first of these was not really new with me. I discovered, like the late C. S. Forester, that I did not know what a novel was. Given the whole sweep of the form in English, from *Pamela* to *V*, the closest one can come to labeling it is Forester's definition, "a prose fiction of some length." People who tell you sternly that a fiction of 45,000 words or more that doesn't meet their standards of complication is not, therefore, a novel should perhaps read more widely before opening their mouths. If Forester can't help them, maybe Flaubert or Leonid Andreyev might open their minds.

The second discovery was that "Beep," as Mr. Shaw had seen all along, was *about* something—and something important to me, if not to anyone else. It deserved rethinking and expansion, especially from the perspective of fifteen additional years of brooding about the things it discusses. I had come to some new conclusions about its matter (some of them by myself, some with the help of discussions with the dedicatee, although he appeared rather later in the process) which I thought—I shan't pause for modesty—to be downright urgent.

One way of putting this would be to say that although the book is fiction, the successive and conflicting speculations which it contains about time, knowledge, and free will are all intended to be taken seriously.

There is still not much physical action here, let alone any melodrama. The structure of the story is still nearly as skeletal, indeed nearly perfunctory, as Mr. Sloane held it to be in 1954. I have not "novelized" it by including a batch of new characters or psychological analysis or social comment. There are a number of new episodes, but only those I needed to further the new course of the argument.

Instead, I have tried to make a great deal more out of the speculations that prompted the story in the first place. I had set out to dramatize these speculations in the short version; here, I am still going about that work, I hope more thoughtfully. The drama, for those capable of enjoying it in this form, lies more in the speculations than in the action, just as before.

Science-fiction stories do come out like this sometimes. That is for me one of the several joys of the field. But then, I actively enjoy brooding, rather to the despair of my relatives; and the kind of science fiction I sometimes write out of it—or read into it—is not for everybody. Those who expect fairy chimes, or bloodshed, must this time apply elsewhere. I condemn neither, but I am up to neither here.

—JAMES BLISH

Treetops
Woodlands Road
Harpsden (Henley)
Oxon., England
1970

The principle of causality, for example,—what is it but a postulate, an empty name covering simply a demand that the sequence of events shall some day manifest a deeper kind of belonging of one thing with another than the mere arbitrary juxtaposition which now phenomenally appears? It is as much an altar to an unknown god as the one that Saint Paul found at Athens. All our scientific and philosophical ideals are altars to unknown gods. Uniformity is as much so as is free will. If this be admitted, we can debate on even terms.

—WILLIAM JAMES, *The Dilemma
of Determinism*

PROLOGUE: *A Frame on Randolph*

1

The man code-named Josef Faber—and after ten years he no longer cared about his birth name—lowered his bulky newsfac slightly. Finding the softly pretty young girl on the park bench looking his way, he smiled an agonizingly embarrassed smile and ducked back into the paper again.

Pretty indeed, in a blond sort of way; also, bland with youth and blind with unfocussed expectancy. She'd hardly noticed him; he wasn't the right sort. He was quite certain that he looked the part of a middle-aged, steadily employed, harmless citizen enjoying a Sunday break from the bookkeeping and family routines—hardly the man to fill out a daydream.

He was also quite certain, despite his official instructions, that it wouldn't make the slightest difference had he looked like himself, or like the young Adonis, for that matter. These boy-meets-girl assignments always came off. Jo had never tackled a single one that had really required him.

As a matter of fact, the primitive newspaper, which he was supposed to be using only as a blind, interested him a good deal more than his job did. He had only barely begun to suspect the obvious ten years ago, when the Service for mysterious reasons had snapped him up. Now, after a decade as a field agent, he was still fascinated to see how smoothly the really important situations came off. The *dangerous* situations—not boy-meets-girl.

This affair of the Black Horse Nebula, for example.

Some days ago the papers and the commentators had begun to mention reports of disturbances in that area, and Jo's practiced eye had picked up the mentions. Something big was cooking.

Yesterday it had boiled over—the Black Horse Nebula had suddenly spewed forth ships by the hundreds, a massed armada that must have taken more than a century of effort on the part of a whole star-cluster, a production drive conducted in a dark and distant and difficult-to-observe part of the galaxy, and under the strictest and most fanatical kind of secrecy.

And, of course, the Service had been on the spot in plenty of time. With three times as many ships, disposed with mathematical precision so as to enfilade the entire armada the moment it broke out from the nebula. The battle hadn't even been a massacre; most of the irrupting fleet had found itself so trapped that not even automatic suiciding circuits had been fast enough to prevent surrender. The attack had been smashed before the average citizen could ever even begin to figure out what the attackers might have thought it had been aimed at.

Good had triumphed again over evil.

Of course.

Furtive scuffings on the gravel drew his attention briefly. He looked at his watch, which said 14:58:03. That was the time, according to his instructions, when boy had to meet girl.

He had been given the strictest kind of orders to let nothing interfere with this meeting—the orders always issued on boy-meets-girl assignments. But, as usual, he had nothing to do but observe. The meeting was coming off on the dot, without any prodding or protection from Jo. They always did.

Of course.

With a sigh, he folded his newspaper, smiling again at the couple—yes, it was the right man, too—and moved away, as if reluctant to abandon his bench, but yielding politely all the same to the exigencies of incipient love. He wondered what would happen were he to pull away the false mustache, pitch the newspaper onto the grass, and bound away with a joyous whoop. He suspected that the course of history would not have been deflected by even a second of an arc.

He was not minded to try the experiment, though. For one thing, that was not how he was supposed to earn his pay. For another, only the suspicion that his presence had been totally irrelevant prevented him from feeling like a pimp. So ambiguous a state of mind was an uncomfortable distance from how he had expected a field agent of the Service would feel, ten years ago when he had first been approached. He no longer expected to be asked to meet space pirates in hand-to-hand battle, or to outwit some sinister planetary regent in a diplomatic duel with no reward but a secret promotion and the grateful smile of a princess who, alas, must wed another; but he did not know *why*. He was getting to be a little old for combat or for princesses, but what was worse, he had become a lot more cynical without having become even slightly the wiser.

He had also become pretty damned bored.

The park was pleasant. The twin suns warmed the gravel path and the greenery without any of the blasting heat which one or the other brought to bear later in their separate, epicyclic summers. The people here were candid, friendly, hardworking, obsessed with gardens, all bread and cheese and beer; their idea of adventure was private flying to the next county to look at the scenery. Randolph was altogether the most comfortable planet he had visited in years. More than a little backward, perhaps, but restful, too.

It was also slightly over a hundred light-years away from Earth. It would be interesting to know how Service headquarters on Earth could have known in advance that boy would meet girl at a certain spot on Randolph, precisely at 14:58:03.

Or how Service headquarters could have ambushed with micrometric precision a major interstellar fleet, with no more preparation than a few days' build-up in the newspapers and video could evidence.

The press was free on Randolph, as everywhere. It reported the news it got in any way it chose. Any concentration of Service ships in the Black Horse area, or anywhere else, would have been noticed and reported on. The Service did not forbid such reports for "security" reasons or for any other reasons. Yet there had been nothing to report but that:

(a) an armada of staggering size had erupted with no real warning from the Black Horse Nebula; and

(b) the Service had been ready.

By now, it was commonplace that the Service was always ready. It had not had a defect or a failure in well over two centuries. It had not even had a fiasco, the alarming-sounding technical term by which it referred to the possibility that a boy-meets-girl assignment might not come off.

Jo hailed a hopper. The hell with it. Whatever he had joined the Service for, it had not been to be bored to death. It was time for a showdown.

Once inside the hopper, he stripped himself of the mustache, the bald spot, the forehead creases—all the make-up that had given him his mask of friendly innocuousness—and defied both regulations and anti-litter ordinances by dropping them out the window.

The hoppy watched the whole process in the rear-view mirror. Jo glanced up and met his eyes.

"Pardon me, mister, but I figured you didn't care if I saw you. You must be a Service man."

"That's right. Take me to Service HQ, will you?"

"Sure enough." The hoppy gunned his machine. It rose smoothly to the express level. "First time I ever got close to a Service man—far as I know. Didn't hardly believe it at first when I saw you taking your face off. You sure looked different."

"Have to, sometimes," Jo said, preoccupied.

"I'll bet. No wonder you know all about everything before it breaks. You must have a thousand faces each, your own mother wouldn't know you, eh? Don't you care if I know about your snooping around in disguise?"

Jo grinned. The grin created a tiny pulling sensation across one curve of his cheek, just next to his nose. He stripped away the overlooked bit of tissue and examined it reproachfully.

"Of course not. Disguise is an elementary part of Service work. Anyone could guess that. We don't use it often, as a matter of fact—only on very simple assignments."

"Oh." The hoppy sounded slightly disappointed, as melodrama faded. He flew silently for about a minute. Then speculatively he said, "Sometimes I think the Service must have timetravel, the things they pull."

Jo could not have risen to this bait even had he known the answer. He was in fact beginning to feel a slight ebbing of his own bravado.

"Well, here you are. Good luck, mister."

"Thanks." He thought he would need it. Setting his shoulders, he marched directly to Krasna's office.

Krasna was a Randolpher, Earth-trained, and answerable to the Earth office, but otherwise pretty much on his own. His heavy, muscular face wore the same expression of serene confidence that was characteristic of senior Service officials everywhere—even some that, technically speaking, had no faces to wear it.

"Boy meets girl," Jo said briefly. "On the nose and on the spot."

"Good work, Jo. Smoke? Drink? Rax?" He rotated the table beside his desk at Jo with an expansive gesture.

"Nope, not now, thanks. Like to talk to you, if you've got the time."

Krasna pushed a button, and a toadstool-like chair rose out of the floor behind Jo. "All the time in time. What's on your mind?"

"Well," Jo said carefully, "I'm wondering why you patted me on the back just now for not doing a job."

"You did a job."

"I did not," Jo said flatly. "Boy would have met girl, whether I'd been here on Randolph or back on Earth. The course of true love *always* runs smooth. It has in all my boy-meets-girl cases, and it has in all the boy-meets-girl cases of every other field agent with whom I've compared notes."

"Well, good," Krasna said, smiling easily. "That's the way we like to have them run. And that's the way we expect them to run. But, Jo, we like to have somebody on the spot, somebody with a reputation for resourcefulness, just in case there's a snag. There almost never is, as you've observed. But . . . just suppose there were?"

Jo snorted. "If what you're trying to do is establish preconditions for the future, any interference by a Service agent would throw the eventual result farther off the track. I know that much about probability."

"And what, may I ask, makes you think we're trying to set up the future?"

"It's obvious even to the hoppies on your own planet. The one that brought me here told me he thought the Service had time-travel. It's especially obvious to all the individuals and governments and entire populations that the Service has bailed out of serious messes for centuries, with never a single failure." Jo shrugged. "A man can be asked to safeguard only a small number of boy-meets-girl cases before he realizes, as an agent, that what the Service is safeguarding is the future children of those meetings. Ergo—the Service *knows* what those children are to be like and has reason to want their future existence guaranteed. What other conclusion is possible?"

Krasna took out a cigarette and lit it deliberately; it was obvious that he was using a customary maneuver to cloak his response.

"None," he admitted at last. "We have some fore-knowledge, of course. We couldn't have made our reputation with espionage alone. But we have obvious other advantages: genetics, for instance, and operations research, the theory of games, the Dirac transmitter—it's quite an arsenal, and of course there's a good deal of prediction involved in all those things."

"I see that," Jo said. He changed his mind about the cigarette and helped himself to one. "But these things don't add up to infallibility—and that's a qualitative difference, Kras. Take this affair of the Black Horse armada. The moment the armada appeared, we'll assume, Earth heard about it by Dirac and started to assemble a counter-armada. But it takes *finite time* to bring together a concentration of ships and men, even if your message system is instantaneous.

"The Service's counter-armada was *already on hand*. It had been building there for so long and with so little fuss that nobody even noticed it concentrating until a day or so before the battle. Then planets in the area began to sit up and take notice, and be uneasy about what was going to break. But not very uneasy; the Service always wins—that's been a statistical fact for centuries. *Centuries*, Kras. Good Lord, it takes almost as long as that, in straight preparation, to mount some of the campaigns we've pulled off! The Dirac gives us an advantage of ten to twenty-five years in really extreme cases out on the rim of the Galaxy, but no more than that."

He realized that he had been fuming away on the cigarette until the roof of his mouth was almost scorched, and stubbed it out angrily.

"That's a very different thing," he said, "than knowing in a general way how an enemy is likely to behave, or what kind of children the Mendelian laws say a given couple should have. It means that we've got some way of reading the future in minute detail. That's in flat contradiction to everything I've been taught about probability, but I have to believe what I see."

Krasna laughed. "That's a very able presentation," he said. He seemed genuinely pleased. "I think you'll remember that you were first enticed into the Service when you began to wonder why the news was always good. Fewer and fewer people wonder about that nowadays; it's become a part of their expected environment." He stood up and ran a hand through his hair, a gesture usually preliminary to an interview with some civilian official. "Now you've carried yourself through to the next stage. Congratulations, Jo. You've just been promoted!"

"I have?" Jo said incredulously. "I came in here with the notion that I might get myself fired."

"Quite the contrary. These were questions you had to ask and that I've been waiting to hear. Now, come around to this side of the desk, Jo, and I'll play you a little history."

Krasna unfolded the desk top to expose a holograph tank—a small 3V screen. Obediently Jo rose and went around the desk to where he could see whatever was coming from the front, 3V was of course visible from any side, but proscenium thinking died hard, and he disliked watching people's backs.

Krasna said, "I had a standard indoctrination tape sent up to me a week ago, in the expectation that you'd be ready to see it about now. It's mostly a dramatization, and it pretty well had to be, as you'll see, considering that it covers some events that happened before either of us was born and which weren't recorded at the time. But it's as accurate as we could possibly make it. Ready?"

"You bet. Go ahead."

Krasna touched the board. A small dot of light appeared in the heart of the tank and went out again. At the same time, there was a small *beep* of sound. Then the tape began to unroll and a scene developed within the cube. The set seemed to be an office much like this one, though that had now gone quite dark; but the clothing was definitely period.

"As you suspected," Krasna's voice said conversationally in the dimness, over the rising voices of the actors, "the Service is infallible—within limits. How it got to be that way is a story that started several centuries back."

The Song of the Beep

CHAPTER ONE: *A Little Slip of a Thing*

Dana Lje—her father had been a Hollander, her mother born in the Celebes—sat down in the chair that Captain Robin Weinbaum had indicated, crossed her legs, and waited, her blue-black hair shining under the lights.

Weinbaum eyed her quizzically. The conqueror Resident who had given the girl—or, more likely, her grandmother—her entirely European name had been paid in kind, for his descendant's beauty had nothing fair and Dutch about it. To the eye of the beholder, Dana Lje seemed a particularly delicate virgin of Bali, despite her Western name, clothing, and assurance. The combination had already proved to be piquant for the millions who watched her television column, and Weinbaum found it no less charming at first hand. Also, she was swinging her free foot slightly, which in a less sophisticated woman would have been a para-taxical sign that she had designs on the man she was talking to. Regretfully, he decided not to believe it.

"As one of your most recent victims," he said, "I'm not sure that I'm honored, Miss Lje. A few of my wounds are still bleeding. But I am a good deal puzzled as to why you're visiting me now. Aren't you afraid I'll bite back?"

"I had no intention of attacking you personally, and I don't think I did," the video columnist said seriously. "It was just pretty plain that our intelligence had slipped badly in the Erskine affair. It was my job to say so. Obviously you were going to get hurt, since

27

you're the head of the bureau—but there was no malice in it."

"Cold comfort," Weinbaum said dryly. "But thank you, nevertheless."

The Eurasian girl shrugged. "That isn't what I came here about, anyway. Tell me, Captain Weinbaum, have you ever heard of an outfit calling itself Interstellar Information, Limited?"

Weinbaum shook his head. "Sounds like a skiptracing firm. Not an easy business, these days."

"That's just what I thought when I first saw their letterhead," Dana said. "But the letter under it wasn't one that a private-eye outfit would write. Let me read part of it to you."

Her slim fingers burrowed in her inside jacket pocket, and emerged again with a single sheet of paper. No letterhead, plain typewriter bond, Weinbaum noted automatically; therefore she had brought only a transcript with her, not even a photocopy, and had left the original letter in some very safe place. The copy, then, would be incomplete—probably seriously.

"It goes like this: *Dear Miss Lje: As a syndicated video commentator with a wide audience and heavy responsibilities, you need the best sources of information available. We would like you to test our service, free of charge, in the hope of proving to you that it is superior to any other source of news on Earth. Therefore, we offer below several predictions concerning events to come in the Hercules and the so-called 'Three Ghosts' areas. If these predictions are fulfilled one hundred percent—no less— we ask that you take us on as your correspondents for those areas, at rates to be agreed upon later. If the predictions are wrong in any respect, you need not consider us further.*"

"Humm," Weinbaum said slowly. "They're confidant cusses, aren't they? But the dodge is an old one, Miss

Lje. Let's suppose I wanted to start such a racket. I would pick twelve commentators, or millionaires, or whatever, and send them predictions on two events with only two possible outcomes, covering among them all the possibilities—two yesses, two no's, two combinations of yes and no. Then I would await the actual outcomes and send one yes-or-no prediction to the two men who had gotten the predictions that both turned out right. Finally, I would approach the sole survivor, who by now is convinced that I am indeed infallible, with a proposition that he sink all his money in some paper company which I covertly own; and then, of course, I vanish. Millionaires would be better than commentators because there are more of them and one could run a longer series; this outfit must be amateur—maybe even thinks the idea a new one."

"It's new to me," Dana confessed. "But what makes you so sure?"

"Of course I'm not sure. But the odd juxtaposition of logical types in the proposed predictions is almost diagnostic—it makes the whole operation so much harder. The Three Ghosts make up only a little solar system, actually only one inhabited planet, because the 'ghosts' in question are respectively a red giant sun, a dwarf companion, and an only barely substellar gas giant, of which the planet is a satellite: the Styrtis Delta system. On the other hand, the 'Hercules area' could include the entire star cluster—or maybe even the whole constellation, which is a hell of a lot of sky. On the face of it, this outfit seems to be trying to tell you that it has thousands of field correspondents of its own, maybe as many as the government itself. If so, swindle or no swindle, I'll guarantee that they're bragging."

"That may well be so. But before you make up your

mind, let me read you one of the two predictions." The transcript rustled in Dana Lje's hand. *"At* 03 : 16:10, *on Year Day,* 2090, *the Hesstype interstellar liner* Brindisi *will be attacked in the neighborhood of the Three Ghosts system by four—"*

Weinbaum sat bolt upright with an abruptness perilous for an occupant of a swivel chair. "Let me see that letter!" he said, his voice harsh with repressed alarm.

"In a moment," the girl said, adjusting her skirt composedly. "Evidently I was right in riding my hunch. Let me go on reading: *by four heavily armed vessels flying the lights of the navy of Hammersmith II. The position of the liner at that time will be at coded coordinates* 88-*A-theta*-88-*gimel*-8, *code and-per-se-and. It will—"*

"Miss Lje," Weinbaum said, "I'm sorry to interrupt you again, but what you've said already would justify me in jailing you at once, no matter how loudly your sponsors, your network, and the civil rights committees might scream. I know nothing about this Interstellar Information outfit, nor do I know whether or not you did receive any such letter as the one you allege to be quoting. But I will tell you that you've shown yourself to be in possession of information that only yours truly and four other men in the galaxy are supposed to know. It's already too late to tell you that everything you say may be held against you. All I can say now is, it's high time you clammed up!"

"I thought so," she said, apparently not disturbed in the least. "Then that liner *is* scheduled to hit those coordinates, and the coded time coordinate corresponds with the predicted Universal Time. Hence we can scratch the hypothesis of any simple swindle. Is it also true that the *Brindisi* will be carrying a top-secret communications device?"

"Are you deliberately trying to make me imprison you?" Weinbaum said, baring his teeth. "Or is this just a stunt, designed to show me that my own bureau is full of leaks?"

"It could turn into that," Dana admitted. "But it hasn't, yet. Robin, I've been as honest with you as I'm able to be. You've had nothing but square deals from me up to now. I wouldn't yellow-screen you, and you know it. If this unknown outfit has this information, it might easily have gotten it from where it hints that it got it: from the field."

"Impossible."

"Why?"

"Because the information in question hasn't even reached my *own* agents in the field yet—it couldn't possibly have leaked as far as Hammersmith II or anywhere else, let alone to the Three Ghosts system! Letters have to be carried on ships, you know that. If I were to send orders by ultrawave to my Three Ghosts agent, he'd have to wait three hundred twenty-four years to get them. By ship, he can get them in a little over two months. These particular orders have been under way to him only five days. Even if somebody has read them on board the ship that's carrying them, they couldn't possibly be sent on to the Three Ghosts any faster than they're traveling now."

Dana nodded her dark head. "All right. Then what are we left with but a leak in your headquarters here?"

"What, indeed," Weinbaum said grimly. "You'd better tell me who signed this letter of yours."

"The signature is 'J. Shelby Stevens.'"

Weinbaum switched on the intercom. "Margaret, look in the business register for an outfit called Interstellar Information, Limited, and find out who owns it, and where."

"Much crash?" said his secretary's voice. "Or is yesterday all right?"

"Well, the less time you waste in clowning—"

"Ouch. Much crash, great chief."

Dana Lje said, "Aren't you interested in the rest of the prediction?"

"You bet I am. Does it tell you the name of this communications device?"

"Yes," Dana said.

"What is it?"

"The Dirac communicator."

Weinbaum groaned and turned on the intercom again. "Margaret, send in Doctor Wald. Tell him to drop everything and gallop. Any luck with the other thing?"

"Yes, sir," the intercom said meekly. "It's a oneman outfit, wholly owned by a J. Shelby Stevens, in a Texas border town called Rico City. It was first registered this year."

"Good girl. Flash the Houston office to arrest him, and get Legal started on an appeal for an injunction to impound his charter."

"Right. What's the charge?"

"The charge?" Weinbaum said. "Violation of the Official Secrets Act. When have we needed anything else? Jump!"

he door to Weinbaum's office swung open and Dr. Wald
came in, all six and a half feet of him. He was extremely
blond and looked awkward, gentle, and not very intelligent. Weinbaum never introduced him to any of his
current girl friends if he could possibly avoid it.

"Thor, this young lady is our press nemesis, Dana Lje,
I don't have to tell you, by the look on your face. Dana,
Doctor Wald is officially our chief engineer, unofficially
our director of research. He is also the inventor of the
Dirac communicator, about which you have so damnably
much information."

"It's out *already*?" Dr. Wald said, scanning the tiny
girl with grave deliberation.

"It is, and lot more—*lots* more. Dana, I think you're
a good girl at heart, and for some reason I trust you,
stupid though it is to trust anybody in this job. I should
detain you until Year Day, videocasts or no videocasts.
Instead, I'm just going to ask you to sit on what you've
got until further notice, and I'm going to explain why."

"Shoot."

"I've already mentioned how slow communication is
between star and star. We have to carry all our messages
in ships, just as we did locally before the invention of
the telegraph. The Haertel Drive lets us beat the speed
of light, for ships, but not by much of a margin over
really long distances. Do you understand that?"

"Certainly," Dana said. She appeared a bit nettled,
and Weinbaum decided to give her the full dose at a

more rapid pace. After all, she could be assumed to
better informed than the average layman.

"What we've needed for a long time, then," he sai
"is some virtually instantaneous method of getting
message from somewhere to anywhere. Any time lag,
matter how small it seems at first, between transmissic
and reception has a way of becoming major as longer ar
longer distances are involved. Sooner or later we mu
have this instantaneous method, or we won't be able
get messages from one system to another fast enough
hold our jurisdiction over outlying regions of space."

"Wait a minute," Dana said. "I'd always understoc
that ultrawave is faster than light."

"Effectively it is; physically it isn't. You don't unde
stand that?"

She shook her dark head.

"In a nutshell," Weinbaum said, "ultrawave
radiation, and all radiation in free space is limited to t
speed of light. The way we hype up ultrawave is to u
an old application of wave-guide theory, whereby t
real transmission of energy is at light speed, but a qua
imaginary thing called phase velocity is going fast
But the gain in speed of transmission isn't much.
ultrawave, for instance, we get a beamed message
Alpha Centauri in one year instead of nearly fo
Practically, that's not a very useful gain even over th
short a distance. We need *speed*."

"Can't it be made to go any faster?" she said, frowni

"No. Think of the laser pipe between here a
Centaurus III as a caterpillar. The caterpillar hims
is moving along quite slowly, just at the speed of lig
But the pulses, the waves of contraction, which p
along his body are going forward in the same directi
faster than he's going as a whole—and if you've e

34

watched a caterpillar, you'll know that that is in fact the case. Now if the caterpillar is endless—tail on Earth, head on Centaurus III—and we impose pulse modulation on those waves, we can get the message carried by the modulation there faster than the caterpillar himself would have gotten there.

"Thor here tells me that dimensional analysis shows that this shouldn't work at all, but it does. But there's a physical limit to the number of pulses that can travel along that hard-working caterpillar, and we've already reached that limit. We've taken phase velocity right out to its end point, which is roughly twenty-five percent faster than the speed of light. And we were able to do that much only because it wasn't energy we were transmitting, that remained constant, but information. Clear so far?"

"I think so. When I don't understand, I'll whimper."

"Okay. Obviously, twenty-five percent is no effective gain at all over interstellar distances; ships remain still faster. For a long time, our relativity theories discouraged hope of any improvement. Even the high-phase velocity of a guided wave didn't contradict those theories—it just found a limited, mathematically irrelevant loophole in them. But when Thor here began looking into the question of the velocity of propagation of a Dirac pulse, which is not an energy transfer system at all in any usual sense, he found the answer. The communicator he developed from this does seem to act over long distances, any distance, instantaneously—and it may wind up knocking relativity into a cocked hat. If I don't explain further, you'll understand why."

The girl's face was a study in stunned realization. "I'm not sure I've taken in all the technicalities," she said. "But if I'd had any notion of the political dynamite in this thing—"

"—you'd have kept out of my office," Weinbaum said grimly. "A good thing you didn't. The *Brindisi* is carrying a model of the Dirac communicator out to the periphery of human exploration—the Three Ghosts system—for a final test. The ship is supposed to get in touch with me from out there at a given Earth time, which we've calculated very elaborately to account for the residual Lorentz and Milne transformations involved in overdrive flight, and for a lot of other time phenomena that wouldn't mean anything at all to you.

"If that signal arrives here at the predicted Earth time, then—aside from the havoc the news will create among the few theoretical physicists whom we decide to let in on it—we will really have our instantaneous communicator, and can include all of occupied space in the same time zone. And we'll have a virtually insuperable advantage over any lawbreaker who has to resort to ultrawave locally, and to letters carried by ships over the really long hauls."

"Not," Thor Wald said with a sort of sad sweetness, like Sauerbraten gravy, "if the secret has already found its way into other hands."

"That, of course, is the next question," Weinbaum said. "It still remains to be seen just how much of it *has* leaked. The principle is more than a little esoteric, Thor, and the name of the thing alone is largely honorific and wouldn't mean much by itself even to a trained scientist . . . though I'm beginning to wish we'd called it the Poohsticks communicator anyhow. I gather that Dan's mysterious informant didn't go into technical details about the construction of the device itself . . . or did he?"

"No," Dana said. "I got no engineering details from him at all, let alone any theory."

"Tell the truth, Dana. I know that you're suppressing some of that letter. I can smell blanks in crucial information a mile away. Hell, you haven't even read me the man's second prediction yet."

The reporter shifted her position slightly in the chair. "All right—yes, I am suppressing some of it. But nothing in the least bit technical. There's another part of the first prediction that lists the number and class of ships you'll send to protect the *Brindisi*—the prediction says they'll be sufficient for the job, by the way—and I'm keeping that to myself, to see whether or not it comes true along with the rest. If it does, I think I've hired myself a legman."

"If it does," Weinbaum said, "what you'll have hired for yourself will be a jailbird. Then we'll see how much mind-reading Mister J. Whasit Stevens can do from the subcellar of Fort Butner."

He arose and ushered her out with what he hoped was controlled politeness. This conversation had been a severe strain in a good many more ways than he could have anticipated. The minute the door had closed behind her, he swung on Thor Wald.

"This is very bad," he said. "We'll just have to hope that this Stevens has gotten his information by some conventional means, miracle though that would be all by itself. I can see only three other possibilities. One is that a Dirac message can after all be picked up by some other kind of apparatus."

"Well, I won't risk saying that's impossible," Wald said. "But it's about as likely as making an audio tape of a smoke signal. I think you would save yourself effort to rule that one out."

"The second is that this Stevens has a genuine, independent method of predicting the future. I'll rule that one out all by myself. If he did, he wouldn't be using it in this way. The third is that he has somehow gotten from us enough information to build a Dirac machine of his own."

"You have left out the most important possibility of all."

"I have? What's that?"

"That he has independently *discovered* the communicator."

"Dear God," Weinbaum said. "How likely is that?"

"It's almost completely unlikely. But my dear Robin, likelihood has almost nothing to do with the matter. What counts is the state of the art, plus insight. I invented this machine? Very well, I live in my times—and I am not the only smart cookie who does. The history of science is full of such coincidences, regardless of what the probabilities say."

"Yes ... I remember a few myself. So it all comes down to police work in the end, after all. We've got to find Stevens—and *fast*."

The age of Dun and Bradstreet, of F.B.I. dossiers bulging with anonymous gossip, of legalized wiretapping, of Social Security numbers, of universal credit cards, of coded addresses and telephone numbers and income tax returns (Federal, state, city), and finally of an almost completely computerized bureaucracy had done its work: On the one hand, privacy was now hedged about by the most complex maze of laws in legal history, so complex indeed that violations cases took Jarndycean lifetimes to try, and in all ordinary situations the laws had been replaced by an only slightly less complex code of manners; and on the other, there was no one in the world who had any privacy from Captain Robin Weinbaum of Security Service, when he deemed the situation an emergency, which was seldom, and was sure of his legal grounds, which was usually.

This was an emergency; but his first finding was that J. Shelby Stevens had no past whatsoever.

This in itself did not surprise him, in one sense, for the first step for anyone attempting anything even faintly illegal in this day and age was to adopt an alias, and meddling classified information was certainly a good deal more than faintly illegal. And yet in another sense it did surprise him; Weinbaum always anticipated high intelligence in his opponents—he got fewer rude shocks that way—and he would have thought that any man with the brains to try to set up as enormous an operation as Interstellar Information appeared to be (or was trying

to pass itself off as) would know that Weinbaum's burea[u]
could penetrate any imaginable alias with the spee[d]
and facility of a pin bursting a balloon. If J. Shelb[y]
Stevens did not want to work with the Government, [it]
would have been much more sensible for him to hav[e]
operated in the open under his own name, surrounde[d]
by the hundreds of legal safeguards a really good priva[te]
lawyer could set up for him, and either patiently abi[de]
or legally fend off the questions the bureau would i[n]
evitably ask him.

It was obvious that Stevens did not want to work wi[th]
the Government, for all the first, polite formal inquiri[es]
directed to him were answered by variations of th[e]
maddening letter which is usually the prerogative [of]
Government officials: "Thank you for your letter [of]
November 15th. Mr. Stevens is presently out of town [on]
business, but I shall call your letter to his attention wh[en]
he returns." Routine field work in Rico City showed th[at]
he was indeed not in his offices, and that nobody the[re]
knew where he was. To put the matter more blunt[ly]
he had vanished.

It was not supposed to be possible to vanish under t[he]
multifaceted eye of Captain Robin Weinbaum, b[ut]
Stevens had managed it. There were no existing pho[to]
graphs of him, nor any existing signatures—he paid [his]
bills in cash, in itself so extraordinary a procedure th[at]
it should have made tracing the source or sources of t[he]
money as easy as following a dog to its kennel, but no[t a]
single such note proved to have any useful histo[ry].
Interstellar Information appeared to have no oth[er]
officers to be questioned; indeed, it had no staff at a[ll,]
at least in Rico City, except for one secretary, who prov[ed]
to be about as stupid as it was possible for a secretary [to]
be in these days of robot transcribers.

Weinbaum, who knew that his understanding of the recesses of the female mind was less than perfect, sent Margaret Soames to Rico City to check on the girl, and Margaret reported her to be just what she appeared to be: a genuinely dumb blonde, the kind that thinks Betelguese is something Indians use to darken their skins. There was, Margaret further reported, no possibility that she could be faking it; nor did her background turn up anything in the least useful. She had been hired off the street, without the interposition of any employment agency, and all she knew about J. Shelby Stevens was that he was a little strange, but all the same, "such a sweet old man." Pressed for a description of J. Shelby Stevens, she gave a description of a sweet old man— apparently *quite* an old man, but without further details. Did his letters tell her anything about his business? No, he had only dictated one so far, the one to be sent to Robin Weinbaum or anybody else who called while he was away. Hadn't he also given her one to Dana Lje? Oh no, that must have been before her time; she would remember because she watched Dana Lje's program a whole lot.

And most extraordinary of all, a check upon the corporate status of Interstellar Information showed that it had been provided with no repeat no legal safeguards beyond those that the ordinary citizen could expect in the body of the law. Nor were there any special security precautions set up in the Rico City offices; Weinbaum's field operatives, armored to the teeth against all possible booby-traps and equally well armed to crack the most ingenious safe, found the offices more open to surreptitious search than an ordinary bookie joint would be. The search produced no incriminating letters or indeed any letters at all, no clue as to Stevens's source of income, no list or code table that might lead the bureau to a line on Stevens's field staff, and above all, no trace of Stevens's identity. The offices had been tenanted by another firm up until a little over a month ago; the place was a mass of fingerprints, but there was no way to tell which set, if any, belonged to Stevens.

There simply could not be any such person on Earth. There was only one conclusion possible: Stevens was an Erskine operative, without any previous Earthly history, but with the colossal gall—and, Weinbaum had reluctantly to admit, the even more colossal skill—to attempt a plot of enormous and obviously still hidden complexities with nothing but the bare bones of his unknowable idea. Under such circumstances, the boldness of his approach to Dana Lje was both breathtaking and insulting; his intent, probably disruptive.

Weinbaum ordered a twenty-four-hour Dinwiddie watch on the Rico City offices from the second storey of a tamale parlor across the street in case Stevens should show up again, and had the secretary tailed within the limits of the law; but the secretary did not meet with any old men, or anybody who might be disguised as an old man, nor did any such show up at the offices. He could not impose any such watch on Dana Lje— that would have involved him with the laws protecting freedom of the press, which were almost as ferocious as those protecting privacy—but officially, at least, Dana Lje did not hear anything further from Stevens either, although at Weinbaum's instructions she had offered to accept Stevens's tentative contract. An intensive check of all known Erskine operatives both on and off Earth proved equally unrewarding; they were all accounted for; this had to be a newcomer—perhaps Weinbaum's counterpart himself, a man whose identity was unknown even to his underlings.?

In the end, Weinbaum was forced to a public admission of his incompetence: he issued an appeal to J. Shelby Stevens to produce himself.

Within twenty-four hours, he had an answer. It was a wirefax message that had been dictated from a primitive telephone booth in Rico City and paid for in coin—lots of coin. It read:

MY TIME LIMITED BUT READY TO MEET WITH YOU WITHIN NEXT 24 HOURS. WILL PLACE SELF UNDER STOOLIE'S ARREST VICTORIA CITY JAIL 0200 TOMORROW AND AWAIT YOUR PLEASURE. J. SHELBY STEVENS

"Stoolie's arrest" was a slang technical term for a most complex legal situation under which a citizen volunteered cooperation and information to the Government under complete protection against self-incrimination, even should his information implicate him in a major crime. Furthermore, Stevens had chosen his jail and his time very well; it would be impossible to muster a proper technical crew to make the limited personal study of Stevens which the law allowed and still get there—"there" being in Australia—before Stevens would be released on his own recognizance. All Weinbaum would be allowed would be a secretary—which would, of course, be Margaret Soames, a trained observer; and all that he could contrive to take with him illegally would be a button camera too small to be loaded with color film and filters, and a button recorder too small to produce useful voice spectra.

Clearly, Stevens knew exactly what he was doing. But so, ordinarily, did Captain Robin Weinbaum. Stevens had had the daring to present himself to the jaws of Security. He would escape them this time, there was no possible doubt about that; but he could not possibly escape without leaving behind a residuum of information that the bureau could put to good use. His boldness was admirable; but the times were very hard on freelancers.

Nevertheless, Weinbaum was disquieted. Stevens's expertise was unusual, but not unprecedented. What was impossible was what he had already shown he *knew*.

CHAPTER FOUR: *A Free Prediction*

The Victoria jail was a proper horror. Weinbaum would not have been surprised to find that Stevens had been put into some equivalent of a Dallas jail's drunk tank, and was a little relieved to find instead that he had been put in solitary. However, when he let himself and Margaret into Stevens's cell, locking the door behind them and passing the keys out to the guard, he was upset all over again, for there was so little light in here that the button camera was going to be almost useless.

He sat down heavily on the nearest stool and studied Stevens as best he could. Stevens in turn smiled the weak, benevolent smile of the very old, and laid his book aside on the bunk. The book, Weinbaum knew—since his office had cleared it—was only a volume of pleasant, harmless lyrics by a New Dynasty poet named George Macbeth. Similarly, Stevens had refused to be finger-printed, voice-printed, have his retinal eyeprints photographed, or undergo any other sort of standard identification procedure, as was his privilege as a self-surrendered stoolie. And he was wearing gloves. On him they looked quite in character, for all the difference that made.

"For someone who wants to cooperate with us," Weinbaum said, "your methods are rather extreme, Mr. Stevens."

"No, they are quite standard, as I am sure you know," Stevens said. His voice was high and musical, rather like that of a boy soprano. "I did come here to help you, and I trust you will give me credit for that. Otherwise, let us part friends, and that will be the end."

Weinbaum was momentarily baffled. "All right, thank you for small favors. Now let's get down to business. What *did* you come here to offer me?"

"Were our predictions correct, Captain?" Stevens said.

"I thought I was supposed to be asking the questions. But, again, all right, they were. You still won't tell us how you did it, I presume?"

"But I already have," Stevens protested, "through Dana Lje, as I am sure you also know. Our intelligence network is the best in the universe, Captain. It is superior even to your own excellent organization, as events have shown."

In the background, Margaret Soames's pen raced silently over her pad. If Stevens took any notice of her at all, he gave no sign of it.

"Its results are superior, that I'll grant," Weinbaum said glumly. "If Dana Lje had thrown your letter down her disposal chute, we would have lost the *Brindisi* and our Dirac transmitter both. Incidentally, did your original letter predict accurately the number of ships we would send?"

Stevens nodded pleasantly, his neatly trimmed white beard thrusting forward slightly in the gloom as he smiled.

"I was afraid so." Weinbaum leaned forward. "Do you have the Dirac transmitter, Stevens?"

"Of course, Captain. How else could my correspondents report to me with the efficiency you have observed?"

"Then why don't our receivers pick up the broadcasts by your agents? Dr. Wald says it's inherent in the principle that Dirac casts are picked up by *all* instruments tuned to receive them, bar none. And at this stage of the game, there are so few such broadcasts being made that we'd be almost certain to detect any that weren't coming from our own operatives."

"I decline to answer that question, if you'll excuse the impoliteness," Stevens said, his voice quavering slightly. "I am an old man, Captain, and this intelligence agency is my retirement venture, into which I have invested all my savings. If I told you how we operated, we would no longer have any advantage over your own Service, except for the limited freedom from secrecy which we have. I have been assured by competent counsel that I have every right to operate a private investigation bureau, properly licensed, upon any scale that I may choose; and that I have the right to keep my methods secret, as the so-called 'intellectual assets' of my firm. If you wish to use our services, well and good. We will provide them, with absolute guarantees on all information we furnish you, for an appropriate fee. But our methods are our own property."

Robin Weinbaum smiled twistedly. "I'm not a naïve man, Mr. Stevens," he said. "My Service is hard on naïveté. You know as well as I do that the Government can't allow you to operate on a freelance basis, supplying top-secret information to anyone who can pay the price, or worse, free of charge to video columnists on a 'test' basis, even though you arrive at every jot of that information independently of espionage—which I still haven't entirely ruled out, by the way. If you can duplicate this *Brindisi* performance at will, we will have to have your services exclusively. In short, you will have to become a hired civilian arm of my own bureau."

"Quite," Stevens said, returning the smile in a fatherly way. "We anticipated that, of course. However, we have contracts with other governments to consider: Erskine, in particular. If we are to work exclusively for Earth, necessarily our price will include compensation for renouncing our other accounts."

"Why should it? Patriotic public servants work for their government at a loss, if they can't work for it any other way."

"I am quite aware of that. I am quite prepared to renounce my other interests. But I do require to be paid."

"How much?" Weinbaum said, suddenly aware that his fists were clenched so tightly that they hurt.

Stevens appeared to consider, nodding his flowery white poll in senile deliberation.

"My associates would have to be consulted. Tentatively, however, a sum equal to the present appropriation of your bureau would do, pending further negotiations."

Weinbaum shot to his feet, eyes wide. "You old buccaneer! You know damned well that I can't spend my entire appropriation on a single civilian service! Did it ever occur to you that most of the civilian outfits working for us are on cost-plus contracts, and that our civilian executives are being paid just a credit a year, by their own choice? You're demanding nearly two thousand credits an hour from your own government, and claiming the legal protection that the Government affords you at the same time, in order to let those fanatics on Erskine run up a higher bid!"

"The price is not unreasonable," Stevens said. "The service is worth the price."

"That's where you're wrong! We have the inventor of the machine working for us. For less than half the sum you're asking, we can find the application of the device that you're trading on—of that you can be damned sure."

48

"May I point out that the device has a minimum of
o independent inventors? You are entering upon a
ngerous gamble, Captain."

"Perhaps. We'll soon see!" Weinbaum glared at
e placid face. "I'm forced to let you remain a free man,
r. Stevens. Even were you not protected by the terms
stoolie's arrest, we've been unable to show that you
me by your information by any illegal method. You
d classified facts in your possession, but no classified
cuments, and it's your privilege as a citizen to make
esses, no matter how educated.

"But we'll catch up with you sooner or later. Had
u been reasonable, you might have found yourself
a very good position with us, your income as assured
any political income can be, and your person respected
the hilt. Now, however, you're subject to censorship—
u have no idea how humiliating that can be, but I'm
ng to see to it that you find out. There'll be no more
wsbeats for Dana Lje, or for anyone else."

'Illegal."

'It is indeed illegal—but don't you think the Govern-
nt also has lawyers? Barratry is a deadly weapon
a government's hands. We can tie you in so many
ots that—well, as you yourself point out, Mr. Stevens,
u're an old man. If you bring suit against us, you
l probably win it—probably a minimum of fifteen
rs after you are dead. In the meantime, until you
nage to get a restraining order, I want to see every
rd of copy that you file with any client outside the
reau. Every word that is of use to me will be used,
l you'll be paid the statutory one cent a word for it—
same rate that the F.B.I. pays for anonymous gossip.
erything that I *don't* find useful will be killed without
arance. Eventually we'll have the modification of

the Dirac that you're using, and when that happens, you
be so flat broke that a pancake with a harelip could s₁
right over you."

Weinbaum paused for a moment, astonished at h
own fury.

Stevens's clarinetlike voice began to sound in t
windowless cavity. "Captain, I have no doubt that y
can do this to me, at least incompletely. But it will pro
fruitless. I will give you a prediction, at no charge.
is guaranteed, as are all our predictions. It is this: *
will never find that modification.* Eventually, I will give
to you, on my own terms, but you will never find
for yourself, nor will you force it out of me. In the mea
time, not a word of copy will be filed with you; f
despite the fact that you are an arm of the Governme
I can well afford to wait you out."

"Bluster," Weinbaum said.

"Fact. Yours is the bluster—loud talk based on nothi
more than a hope. I, however, *know* whereof I spe
But let us conclude this discussion. It serves no purpo
you will need to see my points made the hard w
Thank you for granting me my freedom. We will t
again under different circumstances on—let me s
ah, yes, on January 9th of the year 2091. That year
I believe, almost upon us."

Stevens picked up his book again, nodding at We
baum, his expression harmless and kindly, his han
showing the marked tremor of *paralysis agitans*. Weinba
moved helplessly to the door, gesturing to Marga
and flagged the turnkey. As the bars closed behind the
Stevens's voice called out:

"Oh, yes, and a Happy New Year, Captain."

CHAPTER FIVE: *No News Is Bad News*

Weinbaum sent Margaret home, and then went back by himself by way of Rico City, just in case his field operatives had turned up anything new, or in the case Stevens should have made the mistake of checking in back there himself. But, of course, there was nothing.

Weinbaum then blasted his way back into his own home office, at least twice as mad as the proverbial nest of hornets, and at the same time rather dismally aware of his own probable future. If Stevens's second prediction turned out to be as phenomenally accurate as his first had been, Captain Robin Weinbaum would soon be peddling a natty set of second-hand uniforms.

He glared down at Margaret as he went by her desk. She glared right back; she had known him too long to to be intimidated.

"Anything?" he said.

"Dr. Wald's waiting for you in your office. There's one field report—just came in—and a couple of Diracs on your private tape. Any more luck with the old codger?"

"That," he said crushingly, "is Top Secret."

"Proof. That means that still nobody knows the answer out J. Shelby Stevens."

He collapsed suddenly. "You're so right. That's just what it does mean. But we'll bust him wide open sooner or later. We've *got* to."

"You'll do it," Margaret said. "Anything else for me?"

"No. Tip off the clerical staff that there's a half-holiday today, then go take in a steak or a stereo or

51

something yourself. Dr. Wald and I have a few private wires to pull ... and unless I'm sadly mistaken, a private bottle of aquavit to empty."

"Right," the secretary said. "My transcribed notes are on your desk. Tie one on for me, chief. I understand that beer is the best chaser for aquavit—I'll have a case sent up."

"If you should return after I am suitably squiffed," Weinbaum said, feeling a little better already, "I will kiss you for your thoughtfulness. *That* should keep you at your stereo at least twice through the third feature."

As he went on through the door of his private sanctum, she said demurely behind him, "It certainly should."

As soon as the door closed, however, his mood abruptly became almost as black as before. Despite his comparative youth—he was now only fifty-five—he had been in the Service a long time, and he needed no one to tell him the possible consequences that might flow from possession by a private citizen of the Dirac communicator. If there was ever to be a Federation of Man in the galaxy, it was within the power of J. Shelby Stevens to ruin it before it had fairly gotten started. Whether or not Stevens intended any such thing was of course irrelevant; he could not know the stakes. And there seemed to be nothing at all that Weinbaum or anybody else could do about it.

As predicted, Thor Wald was waiting for him, and so was the bottle, which except for its label could have been taken to contain nothing more lethal than water. The physicist, note-pad open beside him, was reading a journal the text of which seemed to be about 75 percent mathematics, which was no surprise; Weinbaum was a little taken aback, however, to see that the other 25 percent was inarguably Chinese.

"Hello, Thor," he said glumly. "Pass the bottle. I didn't know Chinese was one of your languages."

"It isn't, not one word," Wald said. "But I don't have to speak it to be able to read it. I can go directly from the ideographs into any of the European languages I do know. It's awfully helpful that the written character for 'horse' is a picture of a horse, the word for 'woman' is a mouth with a roof above it, and so on. When I get into trouble, I can usually guess the meaning from the context of the math—I'd be no good at all with poetry."

"You are a solid mass of surprises. I wish I had a few in exchange."

"I gather it went badly, Robin. Tell me about it."

Briefly, Weinbaum told him. "And the worst of it," he finished, "is that Stevens himself predicts that we won't find the application of the Dirac that he's using, and that eventually we'll have to buy it at his price. Somehow I believe him—but I can't see how it's possible. If I were to tell the Congress that I was going to spend my entire appropriation for a single civilian service, I'd be out on my ear within the next three sessions."

"Perhaps that isn't his real price," the scientist suggested. "If he wanted to barter, he'd naturally begin with a price miles above what he actually wants."

"Sure, sure ... but frankly, Thor, I'd hate to give the old reprobate even a single credit if I could get out of it." Weinbaum sighed. "Despite all the restrictions in that damn jail, I smuggled out quite a bit in the way of raw data, but the trouble is, I don't know what to do with it. I've ordered the I.D. lab staff to start with the voice comparator, which is usually pretty sure-fire, but somehow in this case I haven't much hope of its turning up anything."

"How does that work?" Wald said interestedly.

"It's an analog of the blink microscope that astronomers use for discovering new asteroids, comets, and the like. Or new planets, for that matter; Persephone was discovered that way. You put two plates of the same star field, taken at different times, side by side and blink from one to the other; if anything moves, you've got your object. In the same way, the voice comparator isolates inflections on single normally stressed syllables and matches them. It's standard I.D. searching technique, on a case of this kind, but it takes so long that we usually get the quarry by other means before it pays off. In this case, we'll have to compare Stevens's voice with every single person we've got recorded, since we have no suspects. We'll start with the staff of the bureau itself, since the Dirac is involved, and then go on to the Erskine file. After that, I guess we'll just go on at random, maybe starting with the President. Pardon me while I groan a little."

"Here comes the beer. That ought to help some."

"I doubt it. Well, let's see what's come in from the field."

Thor Wald moved silently away from Weinbaum's desk while the officer unfolded it and set up the Dirac screen. Stacked neatly next to the ultraphone—a device Weinbaum had been thinking of, only a few days ago, as permanently outmoded—were the tapes Margaret had mentioned. He threaded the first one into the Dirac and turned the toggle to the position labeled *Start*.

Instantly the whole screen went pure white and the audio speakers emitted an almost instantly end-stopped blare of sound—a *beep* that, as Weinbaum already knew, made up a continuous spectrum from about 15 cycles per second to well above 28,000 c.p.s.; how much farther above had yet to be determined, for it reached well

eyond the limits of any known recording apparatus,
to regions where it killed laboratory animals and set
re to their cages. Then the light and the noise were
ne as if they had never been, and were replaced by
e familiar face and voice of Weinbaum's local
inwiddie ops chief in Rico City.

"There's been no transmission of any kind either into
out of Stevens's offices here," the operative said
ithout preamble. "They're using hardly enough power
keep the lights on, there hasn't been one phone call,
id Stevens's secretary has been spending most of her
ne with the button of a transistor radio in her ear.
'hat she's been getting from that has been commercial
nk, from the station in Acapulco, eighty percent hop-
id-holler and the rest pitches for Genuine Juarez
ld American Scotch. Absolutely *nothing* is going on,
I stake my life on it—the place is a desert. And there's
sign of Stevens at all. Orders?"

Weinbaum dictated rapidly to the blank stretch of
pe that followed: "Margaret, next time you send any
rac tapes in here, cut that damnable beep off them
st. Tell the boys in Rico City that Stevens has been
eased, and that I'm proceeding for an Order in
curity to tap his ultraphones and his vocal lines—this
one case where I'm sure we can persuade the court
it the tap is necessary. Also—and be damn sure you
ie this—tell them to proceed with the tap immedi-
ly and to maintain it whether or not the court okays it;
d ditto with the Dinwiddie monitoring. I will thumb-
nt a Full Responsibility Confession for them. We can't
rd to play patty-cake with Stevens—the potential
nage is just too damn great. And, oh, yes, Margaret,
d the message by courier, and send out general
ers to everybody concerned not to use the Dirac

again except when distance and time rule every oth[e]
medium out. For the time being I prefer to take Stevens[']
claim that he can receive Dirac 'casts as proved."

He put down the mike and stared morosely for [a]
moment at the beautiful Eridanean scrollwood of h[is]
desk top. Wald coughed inquiringly and retrieved t[he]
aquavit.

"Excuse me, Robin," he said, "but I should thi[nk]
that would work both ways."

"So should I. And yet the fact is that we've nev[er]
picked up as much as a whisper from either Steve[ns]
or his agents. I can't think of any way that that cou[ld]
be pulled off, but evidently it can."

"Well, let's rethink the problem, and see what [we]
get," Wald said. "I didn't want to say so in front [of]
the young lady, for obvious reasons—I mean M[iss]
Lje, of course, not Margaret—but the truth is th[at]
the Dirac is essentially a simple mechanism in princip[le.]
As I told you, I seriously doubt that there's any way [to]
transmit a message from it that can't be detected—a[nd]
an examination of the theory with that proviso in mi[nd]
might give us something new."

"What proviso?" Weinbaum said. Thor Wald l[eft]
him behind rather often these days.

"Why, that Dirac transmission doesn't *necessar[ily]*
go to all communicators capable of receiving it. [If]
that's true, then the reason why it is true should eme[rge]
from the theory."

"I see. Okay, proceed on that line. There does[n't]
seem to be any other; as my Rico City op said, everythi[ng]
else is an absolute desert, and that includes Steven[s']
dossier. Prior to the opening of the office in Rico Ci[ty]
there's no dope whatever on J. Shelby Stevens. T[he]
man as good as rubbed my nose in the fact that h[e]

using a pseud when I first talked to him. I asked him what the 'J' in his name stood for, and he said, 'Oh, let's make it Jerome.' But who the man behind the pseud *is*—"

"Is it possible that he's using his own initials?"

"No," Weinbaum said. "Only the dumbest ever do that, or transpose syllables, or retain any connection at all with their real names. Those are the people who are in serious emotional trouble, people who drive themselves into anonymity, but leave clues strewn all around the landscape—those clues are really a cry for help, for discovery. Of course, we're working on that angle—we can't neglect anything—but J. Shelby Stevens isn't that kind of hairpin, I'm sure. In fact— I haven't brought this up before, because it's a graveyard secret—I'm seriously entertaining the possibility that he's actually an entity called a vombis, a totally protean creature working for a sort of empire on the far side of the galaxy called the Green Exarchy. If he is, we've had it, for sure."

"I never heard of either."

"I wish I never had. Forget it for the time being." Weinbaum stood up abruptly. "Pretend I never mentioned it, Thor. In the meantime, what's first on your technical program?"

CHAPTER SIX: *A Cycle of Hoops*

"Well . . . I suppose we'll have to start by checking the frequencies we use. We're going on Dirac's assumption—and it works very well, and always has—that a positron in motion through a crystal lattice is accompanied by de Broglie waves which are transforms of the waves of an electron in motion somewhere else in the universe. Thus if we control the frequency and path of the positron, we control the placement of the electron— we cause it to appear, so to speak, in the circuits of a communicator somewhere else. After that, reception is just a matter of amplifying the bursts and reading the signal."

"Plus collimation, I assume."

Wald scowled and shook his blond head. "No, collimation is not only unnecessary, it's outright impossible. The effect is absolutely non-linear—it doesn't even spread like a wave front, it just occurs everywhere, all at once and at the same time. If Stevens is getting out messages that we don't pick up, my first assumption would be that he's worked out a fine-tuning circuit that's more delicate than ours, and that he's more or less sneaking his messages under ours. The only way that could be done, as far as I can see at the moment, is by something really fantastic in the way of exact frequency control of his positron gun—quite ignoring the fact that your people haven't caught him with as much as a water pistol, thus far. If so, the logical step for us is to go back to the beginning of our tests and re-run

our X-ray diffractions, to see if we can refine our measurements of positron frequencies."

The scientist looked so inexpressibly gloomy as he
offered this conclusion that a pall of hopelessness settled
over Weinbaum in sheer sympathy.

"You don't look as though you expected that to
uncover anything new."

"I don't. You see, Robin, things are different in
physics now than they used to be in the twentieth century.
In those days, it was always presupposed that physics
was limitless—the classic statement was made by Her-
mann Weyl, who said that 'It is in the nature of a real
thing to be inexhaustible in content.' We know now
that that's not so, except in a remote, associational
sort of way. When Haertel proved that there is only
one fundamental particle, that in effect closed the book.
Nowadays, physics is a defined and self-limited science;
its scope is still prodigious, but we can no longer think
of it as endless.

"Thanks to Haertel, this is better established in
particle physics than in any other branch of the science.
Half of the trouble physicists of the last century had
with Euclidean geometry—and hence the reason they
evolved so many complicated theories of relativity—is
that it's a geometry of lines, and thus can be subdivided
infinitely. When Cantor proved that there really is
an infinity, at least mathematically speaking, that
seemed to clinch the case for the possibility of a really
infinite physical universe, too."

Wald's eyes grew vague, and he paused to gulp down
a slug of the licorice-flavored aquavit that would have
made Weinbaum's every hair stand on end.

"I remember," Wald said, "the man who taught
me theory of sets in Princeton, many years ago. He

used to say: 'Cantor teaches us that there are many kinds of infinities. *There* was a crazy old man!'"

Weinbaum rescued the bottle hastily. "So, go on, Thor."

"Oh." Wald blinked. "Yes. Well, what we know now is that the geometry which applies to ultimate particles, like the positron, isn't Euclidean at all. It's Pythagorean— a geometry of points, not lines. Haertel, who I sometimes think must have been God, made that assumption just for the sake of argument when he was seventeen years old, and almost everything that's happened in particle physics since has flown out of it. Once you've measured one of those points, and it doesn't matter what kind of quantity you're measuring, you're down as far as you can go. At that point, the universe becomes discontinuous, and no further refinement is possible. At once you have a workable Unified Field Theory, and both the equivalency principle and the whole of quantum mechanics go out the window, and good riddance, too; philosophically they were always scandalous, as a good many twentieth-century physicists realized at the time, but they felt that they were stuck with them; after all, they did get results. A little of quantum mechanics remains—hence our transmitter— but that's all. The remainders are nothing more than bad dreams, like the Aristotelean spheres, or Isaac Newton's bad clock repairman."

"Philosophy isn't my subject, I'm afraid. Let's get back to measurements, and what we might be able to do."

"Well, that's why I was talking about discontinuity, Robin. Haertel may be all wrong about the nature of the universe—ho, ho, ho—but until he's replaced, I have to say that our positron-frequency measurements have already gotten as far down as they can go. There isn't another element in the universe denser than pergium, which you'll recall is the last of the new metastable elements made by the Alvarez packing process—atomic number 1287, the highest permissible under the scholium. Yet we get the same frequency values by diffraction through pergium crystals that we get through osmium crystals; there's not the slightest difference. I'll bet that if we had the energy to drive our X-rays through a neutron star, which I hope I will never be asked to try, the outcome would be the same.

"So: If J. Shelby Stevens is operating in terms of fractions of those values, then he's doing what an organist would call 'playing in the cracks between the keys'— which is certainly something you can *think* about doing, like trying to grow a mighty oak out of the acorn on top of your neck, but something that's in actuality impossible to do. *Hoop*."

"Hoop?" Weinbaum said.

"Sorry. A hiccup only."

"Oh. Well . . . maybe Stevens has rebuilt the organ?"

"That of course has been done. I myself have heard an organ in the Netherlands, built by a fanatic named Fokker, which is tuned to a thirtyone-tone scale—the same scale proposed by Christian Huygens quite a few scores of decades earlier. The analogy is not too bad a one, now that I think back on it. The instrument sounds like a battery of fire trucks and ambulances in heat and is in itself the best possible demonstration that the Pythagorean musical scale is the natural one. But if J. Shelby Stevens," the physicist added firmly, "has rebuilt the metrical frame of the universe to accommodate a private skip-tracing firm, or even an espionage agency, I for one see no reason why we can't counteract him—*hoop*—by declaring the whole cosmos null and void, and devoting ourselves henceforth to serious drinking."

"All right, all right," Weinbaum said, grinning in spite of himself. "I didn't mean to push your analogy right over the edge—I was just asking. But let's get to work on the tests, anyhow. We can't just sit here and let Stevens get away with everything right down to our trousers. If this frequencies angle turns out to be as hopeless as you picture it, we'll just have to try something else."

"Yes, but what else? That's a very pretty problem in itself." Wald eyed the aquavit bottle owlishly. "But not one I'm up to at the moment. Tell me, have I ever sung you the song we have in Sweden called *Natt och Dag*?"

"Hoop," Weinbaum said in a high falsetto, to his own surprise. "Excuse me. No. Let's hear it."

CHAPTER SEVEN: *A Few Cosmic Jokes*

> To go to the Zen state, you must turn your back on it. In the Void everything disappears, including certainty. At the origin of inner space, you are not only on the map; you are also where the map is.
>
> —JOHN H. CLARK

The computer occupied an entire floor of the Security building, its seemingly identical banks laid out side by side on the floor along an advanced pathological state of Peano's "space-filling curve." At the current business end of the line was a master control board with a large television screen at its center, at which Dr. Wald was stationed, with Weinbaum looking, silently but anxiously, over his shoulder.

The screen itself showed a pattern that, except that it was drawn in green light against a dark gray background, strongly resembled the grain in a piece of highly polished mahogany. Photographs of similar X-ray diffraction patterns were stacked on a small table to Dr. Wald's right; several had spilled over onto the floor.

"Well, there it is," Wald sighed at length. "And I won't struggle to keep myself from saying 'I told you so.' What you've had me do here, Robin, is reconfirm about half of the basic postulates of particle physics—which is why it took so long, even though it was the first project we started." He snapped the screen off. "Haertel was right. There are no cracks between the keys for J. Shelby Stevens to play in. That's definite."

"If you'd said. 'That's flat,' you'd have made a joke," Weinbaum said sourly.

"My English isn't good enough for puns, alas—any more than my Chinese is good enough for poetry."

"Look ... isn't there still a chance of error? If not on your part, Thor, then in the computers? After all, they're set up to work only with the unit charges of modern physics; mightn't we have to disconnect the banks that contain that bias before the machines will follow the fractional-charge searching instructions we gave them?"

"Disconnect, he says," Wald groaned, mopping his brow reflectively. "The bias exists everywhere in the machine, my friend, because it functions everywhere on those same unit charges. It wasn't a matter of subtracting banks; we had to add one with a bias all its own, to correct the corrections the computer would otherwise have applied to the programming. The technicians thought I was crazy. Now, five months later, I've proved it."

"I'm in about the same state. I've turned up a couple of things that are useful, but that I'm none too glad to have found out all the same. For instance, our medical director has been issuing vast orders for phony supplies to a dummy firm, paying for them with bureau checks which he's been banking in his own name in a building-and-loan society somewhere in a box canyon in Utah. I don't know how the hell he imagined he could get away with it, under modern credit-checking systems; my only guess is that he's a goose in human feathers. I've had his license revoked, and given the medical side of Personnel a good wigging to boot, but there seems to be no connection at all between these petty thefts and the Stevens affair."

"What was the other thing?"

"That's more serious. Dana Lje was quite right in suggesting that there might be a top-level leak in my own staff. What's worse, the leak turns out to be my invaluable Margaret Soames. I'm letting that rope pay out; it doesn't appear that Margaret is an Erskine operative in herself, but only a tool, and I'm waiting to see whom it is she's feeding the information to. She's not in contact with any of the known Erskine people on Earth, of that I'm quite sure, and I hope to present her unknown friend with a nasty shock by pretending innocence for the time being."

"That *is* a shock," Wald said gravely.

"Yes. I have no business being Security chief at all; I seem to become more naïve every time I as much as blow my nose. But there might just possibly be some link with Stevens here. The logic of it quite escapes me, but I'm watching. One thing is for sure: Our ex-medical director, now defrocked, as well as fired, is not Stevens and had no tie with him whatsoever. Possibly Margaret's contact is, or does, or possibly not. At the moment all my desk drawers are so full of fog that it's awfully difficult even to find the bottle."

"I know that feeling."

"What about the other technical projects?"

"All done," Wald said. "Some time back, as a matter of fact. The staff and I checked every single Dirac tape received since you released J. Shelby from his Australian pokey, for any sign of intermodulation, marginal signals, patterned static of anything else of the kind. There's nothing, Robin, absolutely nothing. That's our net result, all around."

"Which leaves us just where we started," Weinbaum

said. "All the monitoring projects came to the same dead end; I strongly suspect that Stevens hasn't risked any further calls from his home office to his field staff, even though he seemed confident that we'd never intercept such calls—as we haven't. Even our local wire-tapping hasn't turned up anything except calls by Stevens's secretary, making appointments for him with various clients, actual and potential. Any information he's selling these days he's passing on in person— and not in his office, either, because we've got bugs planted all over that and haven't heard a thing."

"That must limit his range of operations enormously— and cut down the possibility of catching him out," Wald objected.

Weinbaum nodded. "Without a doubt—and ours, too, of course—but he shows no signs of being bothered by it. He can't have sent any tips to Erskine recently, for instance, because our last tangle with that crew came out very well for us, even though we had to use the Dirac to send the orders to our squadron out there. If he overheard us, he didn't even try to pass the word; even though we couldn't have overheard him doing so, we'd have known if he had by the outcome. Just as he said, he's sweating us out—"

Weinbaum paused. "Wait a minute. Here comes the invaluable Margaret." His mouth seemed to fill with acid as he spoke. "And by the length of her stride, I'd say she's got something particularly nasty on her mind."

Margaret had hove into earshot in time to catch the last sentence. "You bet I do," she said, with marked vindictiveness. "And it'll blow plenty of lids around here, or I miss my guess. The I.D. squad has finally pinned down J. Shelby Stevens. And they did it the hard way, with the voice comparator alone."

"The motto of the bureau," Weinbaum said, "is, 'Sometimes something works.' Well, don't stand there like a dummy, Margaret. Who *is* he?"

"You're prepared for a shock, I hope."

"I am," Weinbaum said gently. "It ought to be everybody's standard state of mind around here. Let's cut out all this goddam backing and filling. *Who is he?*"

"'He'," Margaret said, "is your sweetheart of the video waves, Miss Dana Lje."

"They're crazy!" Wald said, staring at her.

Weinbaum came slowly out of his first shock of stunned disbelief. "No, Thor," he said finally. "No, it figures. If a woman is going to go in for disguises, there are always three she can assume convincingly outside her own sex: A young boy, a homosexual, and a very old man. Just as a man with a medium-high voice can take on the role of a butch dyke, if he thinks he needs to. And Dana's an actress; that's no news to us."

"But—but why did she do it, Robin?"

"That's what we're going to find out right now. So we wouldn't get the Dirac modification by ourselves, eh! Well, there are other ways of getting answers besides particle physics. Margaret, do you have a pick-up order out for that girl?"

"No," the secretary said. "This is one chestnut I wanted to see you pull out for yourself. You give me the authority, and I send the order—not before."

"Spiteful child. You may regret the delay. Send it, then, and glory in my gritted teeth. Come on, Thor— let's put the nutcracker on this, and hope it isn't just another horse-chestnut after all."

As they were leaving the computer-room floor, Weinbaum stopped suddenly in his tracks and began to mutter in an almost inaudible voice.

Wald said, "What's the matter now, Robin?"

"Nothing, I hope. I keep being brought up short by those predictions. What's the date?"

"Why—January ninth, 2091, if that matters. Why?"

"It's the exact date that 'Stevens' predicted we'd meet again, dammit! Something tells me that this isn't going to be as simple as it looks."

"What is?" Wald said, raising his eyebrows.

"Nothing, of course. But hope springs eternal in the human spleen."

"And what about Margaret?"

"One problem at a time, dammit; one problem at a time."

CHAPTER EIGHT: *The Courtship of Posi and Nega*

If Dana Lje had any idea of what she was in for—and considering the fact that she was "J. Shelby Stevens" it had to be assumed that she did—the knowledge seemed not to make her at all fearful. She sat as composedly as ever before Weinbaum's desk, smoking her eternal cigarette, and waited, one dimpled knee pointed directly at the bridge of the officer's nose. The knee was a courtesy; that was the year of the frontless skirt.

"Dana," Weinbaum said, "this time we're going to get all the answers, and we're not going to be gentle about it. Just in case you're not aware of the fact, there are certain laws relating to giving false information to a security officer, under which we could heave you in prison for a minimum of fifteen years. By application of the statutes about using communications to defraud, plus various local laws against transvestitism with intent to deceive, pseudonymity ditto, and so on, we could probably pile up enough additional short sentences to keep you in Fort Butner until you really do grow a beard. So I'd advise you most earnestly to open up."

"I have every intention of opening up," Dana said. "I know, practically word for word, how this interview is going to proceed, what information I'm going to give you, just when I'm going to give it to you—and what you're going to pay me for it. I knew all that many months ago. So there would be no point in my holding out on you."

"What you're saying, Miss Lje," Thor Wald said

in a resigned voice, "is that the future is fixed, and that you can read it, in every essential detail."

"Quite right, Doctor Wald. Both those things are true, with certain qualifications. I couldn't have predicted that you'd get to the heart of the matter so quickly—I gather that you have had intensive philosophical as well as scientific training—but as you'll see in due course, that won't turn out to be what either of us regard as 'an essential detail.'"

There was a brief silence.

"All right," Weinbaum said grimly. "Talk."

"All right, Captain Weinbaum, pay me," Dana said calmly.

Weinbaum snorted.

"But I'm quite serious," she said. "You still don't know what I know about the Dirac communicator. I won't be forced to tell it, by threat of prison, or by any other threat. You see, I know for a fact that you aren't going to send me to prison, or give me drugs, or do anything else of that kind. I know for a fact, instead, that you are going to pay me—so I'd be very foolish to say a word until you do. After all, it's quite a secret you're buying. Once I tell you what it is, you and the entire bureau will be able to read the future just as I do, and then the information will be valueless to me."

Weinbaum was completely speechless for a moment. Finally he said, "Dana, you have a heart of purest brass, as well as a knee with an invisible gunsight on it. I say that I'm *not* going to give you my appropriation, regardless of what the future may or may not say about it in your private ear. I'm not going to give it to you because the way my government—and yours, in case you hadn't noticed that—runs things makes such a price impossible. Or is that really your price?"

"It would have been my real price, had it turned out that there was any chance of its being paid. However, there is no such chance, and therefore it has to be regarded as a null alternative. Call it my second choice. My first choice, which means the price I'll settle for, and in fact am going to have to settle for, comes in two parts:

"(a) to be taken into your bureau as a responsible officer; and,

"(b) to be married to Captain Robin Weinbaum."

Weinbaum sailed up out of his chair. He felt as though copper-colored flames a foot long were shooting out of each of his ears.

"Of all the . . ." he began. There his voice again failed him completely.

From behind him, where Thor Wald was standing, came something like a large, Scandinavian-model guffaw being choked into insensibility. Dana herself seemed to be smiling a little.

"You see," she said, "I don't point my best and most accurate knee at every man I meet."

Weinbaum sat down again, slowly and carefully.

"Walk, do not run, to nearest exit," he said. "Women and child-like security officers first. Miss Lje, are you trying to sell me the notion that you went through this elaborate hanky-panky—beard and all—out of a burning passion for my dumpy and underpaid person?"

"Not entirely," Dana Lje said. "I want to be in the bureau, too, as I said. Let me confront you, though, Captain, with a fact of life that doesn't seem to have penetrated to you at all, though obviously it has to Doctor Wald. Do you accept as a fact that I can read the future in detail, and that that, to be possible at all, means that the future is fixed? The question has nothing whatsoever to do with strategy or tactics or politics or passion or any other footling notions of that kind; it is instead one of the seven or eight great philosophical questions that remain unanswered, the problem of whether man has or has not free will. I have already gone a very long distance toward proving that he hasn't, as Doctor Wald saw at once. That's what this whole charade has been about. Will you accept that?"

"Since Thor seems able to accept it, I suppose I can, too—provisionally—very damned provisionally."

"I don't accept it, yet," Wald said. "You have piled up quite a startling series of coincidences, Miss Lje, but I in my turn have seen many painfully constructed tables of random numbers turn out to contain un-suspected periodicities; nature appears to be inherently rhythmic. Hence my acceptance is just as provisional as Robin's is."

"There's nothing provisional about my solution," Dana said firmly.

"Defend it, then," Wald said.

"And defend it to me, while you're at it," Weinbaum said. "Unless I've lost my mind some time back, what we are supposed to be talking about is the Dirac communi-cator—the gimmick. You know something about it that we don't know. What is it?"

"Have it your way," Dana said. "Very well. When I first came upon this—uh, this gimmick—quite a while ago, one of the first things that I found out was that I was going to go through the 'J. Shelby Stevens' masquerade, force myself onto the staff of the bureau, and marry you, Robin. At the time, I was both astonished and completely rebellious. I didn't want to be on the bureau staff; I liked my free-lance life as a video commen-tator. I didn't want to marry you, though I wouldn't have been averse to living with you for a while—say, six months or so; good affairs seldom burn out short of that, and in any case you're more attractive than you seem to think you are. And above all, the masquerade struck me as ridiculous.

"But the facts kept staring me in the face. I *was* going to do all these things. There were no alternatives, no fanciful 'branches of time,' no decision-points that might be altered to make the future change. My future, like yours, Doctor Wald's, and everyone else's, was fixed. It didn't matter a snap whether or not I had a decent motive for what I was going to do; I was going to do it anyhow. Cause and effect, as I could see for myself, just don't exist. One event follows another because events are just as indestructible in spacetime as matter and energy are.

"It was the bitterest of all pills. I had always thought of myself as completely free-wheeling and independent. For that matter, I had always been dedicated—and I mean fiercely dedicated—to the belief that people are responsible for what they do, and that an evil act is the product of an evil man. It will take me many years to swallow it completely, and you, too. Doctor Wald will come around a little sooner, I think.

"At any rate, once I was intellectually convinced that all this was so, I had then to protect my own sanity. I knew that I couldn't alter what I was going to do, but the least I could do to protect myself was to supply myself with motives. Or, in other words, what Freud would have called just plain rationalizations.

"That much, it seems, we're free to do; the consciousness of the observer is just along for the ride through time, and can't alter events—but it can comment, explain, invent, interpret, and sometimes even enjoy. That's fortunate, for none of us could stand going through motions that were truly free of what we think of as personal significances.

"So I used this single freedom to supply myself with the obvious motives. Since I was going to be married to you and couldn't get out of it, I set out to convince myself that I loved you. Now I do. Since I was going to join the bureau staff, I thought over all the advantages that it might have over being a video commentator, and found that they made a respectable list. Those are my motives now.

"But I had no such motives at the beginning. Actually, there are never motives *behind* actions. All actions are fixed. What we call motives evidently are rationalizations by the helpless observing consciousness, which is intelligent enough to smell an event coming—and, since it cannot avert the event, instead cooks up reasons for wanting it to happen . . . or ascribes it to the malice of God or man."

"Wow," Thor Wald said, inelegantly, but with considerable force.

"Either 'wow' or 'balderdash' seems to be called for—and I can't quite decide which," Weinbaum said. "We know that Dana is an actress, Thor, so let's not let ourselves get knocked out of the apple tree quite yet. Dana, you've obviously been saving the *really* hard question for the last, and I insist upon that answer now. That questions is: *How?*

"There are several ways to answer it, of course. For instance what *is* the gimmick? Or, *how* did you arrive at this modification of the Dirac transmitter, and how did it tell you what you're now telling us? Remember, we know your background, where we didn't know that of 'J. Shelby Stevens.' You're not a scientist. There wcre some fairly highpowered intellects among your distant relatives, but that's as close as you come. Now you expect us to accept everything you say by fiat, as though you were an Einstein or a Haertel. Your charade, as you call it yourself, has been masterfully baffling, but one doesn't have to be a scientist or a student of tables of random numbers to know that such things can be rigged, and often have been rigged, and that utterly stupid answers to some of the great philosophical questions have been erected upon far longer chains of coincidences—look at poor old—Rhine, for example."

"Also quite true," Thor Wald said. "I do agree that it would be better, Miss Lje, if you came down off Mount Sinai for a moment and started talking particle physics to us instead."

"I'm going to give you a lot of answers to those questions," Dana Lje said. "Pick the ones you like best. They're all true, but they tend to contradict each other here and there. The one thing I *can't* do is give you an answer in terms of particle physics, because I know just enough about that subject to realize that my ignorance of it is pretty close to being abject.

"To begin with, you're right about my relatives, of course. If you'll check your dossier again, though, you'll discover that those so-called 'distant' relatives were the last surviving members of my family besides myself. When they died, second and fourth and ninth cousins though they were, their estates reverted to me, and among their effects I found a sketch of a possible instantaneous communicator based upon de Broglie-wave inversion. The material was in very rough form, and mostly beyond my comprehension, because I am, as you say, no scientist myself. But I was interested, because communication was my business. I could see, dimly, what such a thing might be worth—and not only in terms of my credit account.

"My interest was fanned by two coincidences—the kind of coincidences that cause-and-effect just can't allow, but which do seem to happen all the same in the world of unchangeable events. Haven't you noticed? There are thirteen million people on Manhattan alone, and yet every time I turn around I see someone I know. I've been all over the world and I run into them everywhere ... I've never been into space, but I wouldn't be a bit surprised to meet somebody on Mars or Storisende or Erskine that I knew when I was nine years old."

"Yes, and a word I learned only yesterday crops up in something I read today," Wald said. "One sees what one recognizes, and then is duly astonished; but nothing is proved by it. What actually did happen?"

"For most of my adult life, I've been in communications industries of one kind or another, mostly branches of video. I had communications equipment around me constantly, and I had coffee and doughnuts with communications engineers every day. First I picked up the jargon, then some of the procedures, and eventually, a little real technical knowledge. Some of the knowledge was very simple, like how to read a circuit diagram; and there was a rough diagram in the material I had inherited. Some of the rest of it couldn't have been gotten in any other way.

"Some other things are ordinarily available to highly educated people like Doctor Wald here, and came to me by accident, in horseplay, between kisses, and a hundred other ways—all natural to the environment of a video network, and especially accessible to someone in that environment who wields a certain amount of power, as I increasingly did. I don't suppose I have to defend the existence of the power to you, Robin; you were complaining of it when we first met."

"How true," Weinbaum said. He found, to his own astonishment, that the "between kisses" phrase did not sit very well in his chest, despite the fact that sexual jealousy—particularly the retrospective kind—had been dying out of the world long before he had been born. He added, with unintentional brusqueness:

"What's the other coincidence?"

"A leak in your own staff."

"Dana, you ought to have that set to music. It's becoming so familiar that it may turn into a cliché and be lost to the world otherwise."

"Suit yourself."

"I can't suit myself," Weinbaum said, a little petulantly. "I work for the Government. Was this leak direct to you?"

Grimly, he felt another coincidence coming, to be piled onto the top of the rest; but he was not going to give Dana Lje the slightest hint or lead toward it. Nevertheless, he felt perfectly, irrationally sure that the jaws of the trap of time were closing steadily.

"Not at first," Dana said. "That was why I kept insisting to you in person that there might be such a leak, and why I finally began to hint about it in public, on my program. I was hoping that you'd be able to seal it up inside the bureau before my first rather tenuous contact with it got lost. When I didn't succeed in provoking you into protecting yourself—remember, back then I was still thinking of human acts in terms of motives and volition—I took the risk of making direct contact with the leak myself. And the first piece of secret information that came to me through it was the final point I needed to put my Dirac communicator together. I asked a friend who on earth Dirac was; he told me about the 1933 Nobel Prize, and sent me to *Principles of Quantum Mechanics*, and then to de Broglie's *Physics and Microphysics*; when I was baffled, which was most of the time, he explained things very patiently. And bingo, all of a sudden I knew what the circuit diagram was supposed to do.

"When the machine was all assembled—my friend helped there, too, though he was too amused at my dabbling to take it seriously—it did more than just communicate. It predicted. And now I can tell you why."

Weinbaum said thoughtfully, "I don't find this very hard to accept, after all, so far. Pruned of the philosophy, it even makes some sense of the 'J. Shelby Stevens' affair. I assume that by letting the old gentleman become known as someone who knew more about the Dirac transmitter than I did, and who wasn't averse to negotiating with anybody who had money, you kept the leak working through you—rather than transmitting sensitive data to unfriendly governments."

"It did work out that way," Dana said. "But that wasn't the genesis or the purpose of the Stevens masquerade. I've already given you the whole explanation of how that came about. It happened because it was going to happen. All other explanations for anything are superfluous. *All* other explanation for *anything*."

"Well, you'd better name me that leak, before the man gets away."

"When the price is paid, not before. It's too late to prevent a getaway, anyhow. In the meantime, Robin, I want to go on and tell you the other answer to your question about how I was able to find this particular Dirac machine secret, whereas you and Doctor Wald didn't. What answers I've given you up to now have been cause-and-effect answers, with which we're all more comfortable. But I want to impress upon you that all apparent cause-and-effect relationships are accidents. There is no such thing as a cause, and no such thing as an effect. I found the secret because I found it; that event was fixed. That certain circumstances seem to explain why I found it, in the old cause-and-effect terms, is irrelevant. Similarly, with all your superior equipment and brains, you didn't find it for one reason, and one reason alone: Because you didn't find it. The history of the future says you didn't."

"I pays my money and I takes no choice, eh?" Weinbaum said ruefully.

"I'm afraid so—and I don't like it one bit better than you do."

"Thor, what's your opinion of all this?"

"It's just faintly flabbergasting," Wald said soberly. "However, it hangs together. The deterministic universe which Miss Lje paints was a common feature of the old relativity theories, and as sheer speculation has an even longer history. I would say that in the long run, Robin, how much credence we place in the story as a whole will rest upon her method of, as she calls it, reading the future. If it is demonstrable beyond any doubt, then the rest becomes perfectly credible—philosophy and all. If it doesn't, then what remains is only an admirable job of acting, plus some metaphysics that, while self-consistent, are not original with Miss Lje."

"That sums up the case as well as if I'd coached you, Doctor Wald," Dan said. "I'd like to point out one more thing. If I can read the future, then 'J. Shelby Stevens' never had any need for a staff of field operatives, and he never needed to send a single Dirac message that you might intercept. All he needed to do was to make predictions from his readings, which he knew to be infallible; no private espionage network had to be involved. There was nobody for you to catch but me."

"I see that," Weinbaum said drily. What he saw, of course, was in fact only the logical force of the proposition, which could only suport, but never prove, its validity. For that he had still another test in mind than the one that Wald had proposed. "All right, Dana, let's put the proposition this way: *I do not believe you.* Much of what you say is probably true, but in totality I believe it to be false. On the other hand, if you're telling even a part of the truth, you certainly deserve a place on the bureau staff—it would be dangerous as hell *not* to have you with us—and the marriage is more or less of a minor matter, except to you and me. You can have that with no strings attached; I don't want to be bought, any more than you would.

"So: If you will tell me where the leak is, we will consider that part of the question closed. I make that condition not as a price, but because I don't want to get myself engaged to somebody who might be shot as a spy within a month. Aiding and abetting, I must tell you, carries the same penalties."

"Fair enough," Dana said. "Robin, your leak is Margaret Soames. She is an Erskine contact, and nobody's bubblebrain. She's not an Erskine operative herself, but as a highly trained technician she's probably just as effective as one."

"Well, I'll be damned," Weinbaum said. He did not have to work very hard to register astonishment. "Then she's already flown the coop—she was the one who first told me that we'd identified you. She must have taken on that job in order to hold up delivery long enough to arrange a getaway."

"That's right. But you'll catch up with her, day after

tomorrow. And you are now a hooked fish, Robin."

There was another suppressed burble from Thor Wald.

"I accept the fate happily," Weinbaum said, eyeing the gunsight knee. "In return, I'll tell you that we already knew about Margaret—I was hoping to use her to trap her opposite number. And she made a nice test case for you, which you passed. Now, if you will tell me how you work your swami trick, and it backs up everything else you've said to the letter, as you claim, I'll see to it that you're also sworn into the bureau and that all charges against you are quashed. Otherwise, I'll probably have to kiss the bride between the bars of a cell."

Dana smiled. "The secret is very simple. It's all in the beep."

Weinbaum's jaw dropped. "The beep? The Dirac noise?"

"That's right. You didn't find it out because you considered the beep to be just a nuisance, and ordered Miss Soames to cut it off all the tapes before sending them in to you. Miss Soames, who had some inkling that the beep was important, was more than happy to do so, leaving the reading of the beep exclusively to 'J. Shelby Stevens,' who she thought was going to take on Erskine as a client."

"Explain," Thor Wald said, looking intense.

"Just as you assumed, every Dirac message that is sent is picked up by every receiver that is capable of detecting it, regardless of distance. *Every* receiver—including the first one ever built, which is yours, Doctor Wald, through the hundreds of them that will exist throughout the galaxy in the twenty-fourth century, to the untold thousands of them that will exist in the thirtieth century, and so on. The Dirac beep is the simultaneous reception of *every one of the Dirac messages that has ever been sent, or ever will be sent.* Incidentally, the cardinal number of the total of those messages is a relatively small and of course finite number; it's far below really large finite numbers such as the number of electrons in the universe, even when you break down each and every message into 'bits' and count those. I have the impression that the use of the instrument in the future is a great deal lower than its potentialities. It seems deliberate, but I have no explanation for it."

"Of course," Dr. Wald said softly. "Of course! But, Miss Lje . . . how do you tune for an individual message? We tried fractional positron frequencies, and got no-where."

"I didn't even know fractional positron frequencies existed," Dana confessed. "No, it's simple—so simple that a lucky layman like me could arrive at it. You tune individual messages out of the beep by time-lag, nothing more. All the messages arrive at the same instant, in the smallest fraction of time that exists, something called a 'chronon.'"

"Yes," Wald said. "The time it takes one electron to move from one energy level to the next. That's the Pythagorean point of time measurement."

"Thank you. Obviously no gross physical receiver can respond to an input that brief, or at least, that's what I thought at first. But because there are relay and switching delays, various forms of feedback and so on in the apparatus itself, the beep arrives at the output end as a complex pulse which has been 'splattered' along the time axis for a full second or more. That's an effect which you can exaggerate by recording the 'splattered' beep on high-speed tape, the same way you would record any event you wanted to study in slow motion. Then you tune up the various failure points in your receiver, to exaggerate one failure and minimize all the others, and use noise-suppressing techniques to cut out the background."

Thor Wald frowned. "You'd still have a considerable garble when you were through. You'd have to sample the messages—"

"Which is just what I did; Robin's little lecture to me about the ultrawave would have given me that hint, if in fact I hadn't been quite familiar with the technique before. I set myself to find out how the ultrawave channel carries so many messages at once, and I discovered that you people sample the incoming pulses every thousandth of a second and pass on one pip only when the wave deviates in a certain way from the mean. Old stuff to me; telephone companies have been doing it for decades. I didn't really believe it would work on the Dirac beep, but it worked out just a well: ninety percent as intelligible as the original transmission after it came through the smearing device. I'd already got enough from the beep to put my plan in motion, of course—but now every voice message in it was available, and crystal clear. If you select three pips every thousandth of a second, you can even pick up an intelligible transmission of music—a little razzy, but good enough to identify the instruments that are playing, and that's a very good test of any communications device."

"Yes, it would be," Thor Wald said. "It would show that you were getting a significant number of the upper partials—the overtones."

"There's a question of detail here that doesn't quite follow," said Weinbaum, for whom the technical talk was becoming a little too thick to fight through. "Dana, you said that you knew the course this conversation was going to take—yet it isn't being Dirac recorded, nor can I see any reason why any summary of it would be sent out on the Dirac afterward."

"That's true, Robin. However, before I leave here, I will make such a transcast myself, on your own office machine. Obviously I will—because I've *already* picked it up on my own Dirac, from the beep."

"In other words, you're going to call yourself up—months ago."

"That's it," Dana said. "It's not as useful a technique as you might think at first, because it's dangerous to make such broadcasts while a situation is still developing. You can safely 'phone back' details only after the given situation has gone to completion, as a chemist might put it."

"That seems to me to be quite a good deal more than a mere question of detail," Thor Wald said. "In fact, it poses a metaphysical problem quite staggering in its implications; I'll need some time to think it through. But do go on, Miss Lje."

"Very well. Once you know, in short, that when you use the Dirac you're dealing with time, you can coax some very strange things out of the instrument."

She paused and smiled.

"I have heard," she said conversationally, "the voice of the president of our galaxy, in 3480, announcing the federaton of the Milky Way and the Magellanic Clouds. I've heard the commander of a world-line cruiser, traveling from 8873 to 8704 along the world-line of the planet Hathshepa, which circles a star on the rim of NGC 4725, call for help across eleven million light-years—but what kind of help he was calling for, or will be calling for, is beyond my comprehension. And many other such things. When you check on me, you'll hear those things, too—and you'll wonder what many of them mean.

"And you'll listen to them even more closely than I did, in the hope of finding out whether or not anyone was able to understand in time to help."

Thor Wald looked quite as dazed as Weinbaum felt. Dana Lje's voice became a little more somber.

"Most of the voices in the Dirac beep are like that—they're cries for help, which you can overhear decades or centuries before the senders get into trouble. You'll feel obligated to answer every one, to try to supply the help that seems to be needed. And you'll listen to the succeeding messages and say: 'Did we—will we get there in time? Did we understand in time?'

"And in most cases you won't be sure. You'll know the future, but not what most of it means. The further into the future you 'travel' with the machine, the more incomprehensible the messages become, and so you're reduced to telling yourself that time will, after all, have to pass by at its own pace, before enough of the surrounding events can emerge to make those remote messages even a little clearer.

"The long-run effect, as far as I can think it through, is not going to be that of omniscience—of our consciousness being extracted entirely from the time stream and allowed to view its whole sweep from one side. Instead, the Dirac in effect simply slides the bead of consciousness forward a certain distance from the present. Whether it's five hundred or five thousand years still remains to be seen. At that point, the law of diminishing returns sets in—or the noise factor begins to overbalance the information, take your choice—and the observer is reduced to traveling in time at the same old speed. He's just a bit ahead of himself, so to speak.

"To a historian, I suppose it will be deeply disappointing that one can't use the beep to look into the past at all. The whole power it gives us quite obviously can date only from the construction of Doctor Wald's first machine. But the powers it does give us I find exciting enough, when I don't find them utterly frightening."

"You've thought a great deal about this," Wald said slowly. "I dislike to think of what might have happened had some less conscientious person stumbled on the secret of the beep."

"That wasn't in the cards," Dana said.

In the ensuing quiet, Weinbaum felt a faint, irrational sense of letdown, of something that had promised more than had been delivered—rather like the taste of fresh bread as compared to its smell, or the discovery that Thor Wald's Swedish "folk song" *Natt och Dag* was only Cole Porter's *Night and Day* in another language. He recognized the feeling: It was the usual emotion of the hunter when the hunt is over, the born detective's professional version of the *post coitum triste*. After looking at the smiling, supple Dana Lje a moment more, however, he was almost content.

"There's one more thing," he said. "I don't want to be insufferably skeptical about this—but I want to see it work. Thor, can we set up a sampling and smearing device such as Dana describes and run a test, within any practicable period?"

"In about half an hour, I would guess," Dr. Wald said. "We have most of the unit already in assembled form on our big ultrawave receiver, and it shouldn't take any effort to add a high-speed tape unit to it. I'll get it done right now."

He went out. Weinbaum and Dana looked at each other for a moment, rather like strange cats. Then the security officer got up, with what he suspected looked like an air of somewhat grim determination, and seized his fiancée's hands, anticipating at least a slight struggle.

That first kiss was, by intention at least, mostly *pro forma*. But by the time Wald padded back into the office, a heavy electronics chassis under each arm, the letter had been pretty thoroughly superseded by the spirit.

CHAPTER NINE: *A Comity of Futures*

The scientist harrumphed and set his gray, crackle-cased burdens on the desk.

"This is all there is to it," he said, "but I had to hunt all through the library to find a Dirac recording with a beep still on it. Just a moment more while I make connections . . ."

Weinbaum used the time to bring his mind back to the matter at hand, although not quite completely. While Wald worked, the scientist added:

"While I was searching, it also occurred to me that we have here an opportunity to throw a large monkey-wrench into the works if we wish to do so. If it worked it would rob the beep of all predictive value—which from the bureau's point of view may turn out to be a desirable thing to do."

"How?" Weinbaum said.

"Miss Lje said she was going to use the office machine to call herself up, back in the past. As far as I can see, it would be simplicity itself to prevent her from doing so. Of course, she could send herself the message later, on her own machine—or, after she is a member of the bureau, on mine—but neither such situation would make an exact match with what she has heard in the beep.

"Would the message in the beep change accordingly? If so, we would after all have an avenue, though perhaps a small one, toward affecting the past. Or if the message stayed the same, it would become inaccurate, and anything else we may hear in the beep would become similarly provisional and dubious."

"Absolutely not," Weinbaum said. "I am not about to authorize the creation of paradoxes at this stage of our ignorance. I want to know what there is to be known, not start tampering with the evidence before I even know what it is."

"Epistemologically sound, I suppose," Wald said; but he looked a little disappointed all the same. The act of *not* performing an experiment did violence to all his best instincts, Weinbaum knew; but he also knew that always giving scientists their heads had lead in the past into some nasty culs-de-sac. And this thing he was dead sure, was as explosive as anything of the kind he had ever encountered.

"In fact," he said, "I want her to make that call right now, before the machine goes temporarily out of service. Dana, step up to the microphone and sing out loud and clear."

Smiling, Dana complied, though she had to be helped with the apparatus; her own, it turned out, was a bread-board rig, while this one was neatly encased. One of its knobs, labeled SYM, baffled her completely.

"What does that do?" she said, pointing.

Thor Wald looked a little embarrassed and at the same time a little amused, like a small boy caught in what he knows is only a minor dereliction.

"Nothing," he said. "It's just that when I got the box onto the transmitter, I discovered I had eight knobs on this side and only seven on the other. So I added one for symmetry, and it's so labeled."

This confession nearly prevented Dana from making the call after all. "Now," she said, "I know why I seemed to be giggling all through what was obviously a dead-serious call. Well, anyhow, it's done. Next patient?"

"I'll just finish the hookup . . . . There now; all ready."

Then two tape spindles began to whir like so many bees, and the end-stopped sound of the Dirac beep filled the room. Wald stopped the recorder, reset it, and started the smearing tape very slowly in the opposite direction. When this process was finished, he reversed again and touched the *Start* button.

A distant babble of voices came from the speaker. Wald frowned and tweedled knobs; the voices faded, but not entirely. As Weinbaum leaned forward tensely, one voice said clearly and loudly above the rest: "Hello, Earth Service. Lieutenant T. L. Matthews at Hercules Station NGC 6341, transmission date 13-22-2091. We have the last point on the orbit-curve of your dope-runners plotted, and the curve itself points to a small system about twenty-five light years from the base here; the place hasn't even got a name on our charts. Scouting shows the home planet to be at least twice as heavily fortified as we had anticipated, so we'll need another cruiser. We have a 'can-do' from you in the beep for us, but we're waiting as ordered to get it in the present. NGC 6341 Matthews out."

After the first instant of stunned amazement—for no amount of intellectual willingness to accept it could have prepared him for the overwhelming fact itself— Weinbaum had grabbed a pencil and begun to write at top speed. As the voice signed out, he threw the pencil down and looked excitedly at Dr. Wald.

"Seven months ahead," he said, aware that he was grinning like an idiot. "Thor, you know the trouble we've had with that needle in the Hercules haystack! This orbit-curve trick must be something Matthews has yet to dream up—at least he hasn't come to me with it yet, and there's nothing in the situation as it stands now that would indicate a closing time of seven months for the case. The computer said it would take three more years."

"It's new data," Dr. Wald agreed solemnly.

"Well, don't stop there, in God's name! Let's hear some more!"

Dr. Wald went through the spinning and tweedling ritual, much faster this time. The speaker said, "Nausentampen. Eddettompic. Berobsilom. Aimkaksetchoc. Sanbetogmow. Datdectamset. Domatrosmin. Vwaptingdorpic. Gummisampel. Out."

"My word," Wald said. "What's all that? It sounds vaguely Slavic. Of course If it's Chinese, I'm properly paid off for my presumption."

"That's what I was talking about," Dana Lje said. "At least half of what you get from the beep is just as incomprehensible. I suppose it's whatever has happened to the English language—or some other language— thousands of years from now."

"No, it isn't," Weinbaum said. He had resumed writing, and was still at it, despite the comparative briefness of the transmission. Suddenly he was back again upon reasonably familiar ground. "Not this sample, anyhow. That, ladies and gentlemen, is code—no language consists exclusively of four-syllable words, of that you can be sure. And the sign-off was clear. What's more, it's a version of our code. I can't break it down very far—it takes a full-time expert to read this stuff—but I get the date and some of the sense. It's March 12, 3022, and there's some kind of a mass evacuation taking place. The message seems to be a routing order."

"But why will we be using code?" Dr. Wald wanted

to know. "It implies that we think somebody might overhear us—somebody else with a Dirac. That could be very messy."

"It could indeed," Weinbaum said. "But very obviously, Thor, we cannot count upon the secret being kept. It's a fact of nature, and as somebody or other remarked long ago, Nature is a blabbermouth; ask the right question, and you'll *always* get the answer. Look how easily Dana found out something that we hadn't, and out of a very limited range of technical information. But we'll find out more about this particular mystery later, I imagine. Give her another spin, Thor."

"Shall I try for a picture this time?"

Weinbaum nodded. A moment later, he was looking squarely into the green-skinned face of something that looked like an animated traffic signal with a helmet on it. Though the creature had no mouth, the Dirac speaker was saying quite clearly:

"Hello, Chief. This, as if you didn't know, is Thammos NGC 2287, transmission date Gor 60, 302 by my calendar, July 2, 2973, by yours. This is a lousy little planet. Everything stinks of oxygen, just like Earth. But the natives accept us and that's the important thing. The effects of the radiation dosage from the nova next door were a hell of a lot worse than the beep had given us to anticipate and we're making repairs correspondingly slowly. But we did find the cub who's supposed to take over from us when he grows up, and get him under shielding; he's sick but safe, unless he's allergic to neutrinos, which would make him a real museum piece, wouldn't it? Detailed report coming later by paw. NGC 2287 Thammos out."

"I wish I knew my New General Catalogue better," Weinbaum said. "Isn't that M 31 in Canis Major, the one with the red star in the middle? And we'll be using non-humanoids there! What *was* that creature, anyhow? It looked like its ancestors had evolved in a puddle of crème de menthe. Never mind, spin her again."

The spindles whirred, and the screen lit to show a view of a widely spaced forest of gigantic missiles, evidently being viewed almost at capsule height, as if from the top of a gantry crane. The camera was slowly scanning. There must have been nearly a hundred of the immense ships, all apparently identical; those nearest the camera were visibly streaked with rust.

From the speaker, a male voice said:

"Service to Rescue. What you see here is the old Kennedy Spaceport, popularly known as the Bone Heap. All of these interplanetary craft simultaneously became obsolete with the discovery of how to travel the Fortean tunnels to the solar and alternate-solar planets. They are all solid-fueled jobs, each powered by a single grain of powder, and an unknown number of them are still functional, after a fashion.

"Burrowes used to pilot one of these things and has known to hang around here a lot lately. We know that Burrowes and his girl friend are holed up in one of them now. The girl's family lodged a complaint with us of possible elopement—which would be none of our business—or even abduction, which would. But what they don't know is that the girl is a confirmed thrill-hunter and an experienced man-trap. At the present moment, she's engaged in goading Burrowes to take one of those crocks off, to show off his prowess. As an ex-hero he's peculiarly susceptible to such an appeal, and he'll yield.

"We have reviewed this tape a dozen times and have never been able to figure out which ship it is, because the actual launching will set off a chain detonation among the other vessels that lost us all visibility, and left this field looking like the back side of the Moon. Thus the problem becomes one of getting Burrowes and the trollop off their flying junkheap before it runs out of propellant or comes apart in mid-air. Remember, once he's airborne, he has very little maneuverability; the ships were essentially ballistic missiles and were capable of no more than two minor course corrections while in the atmosphere."

A low, almost subsonic rumble began to rise under the voice. The camera swiveled wildly. "*There he—*"

The rumble suddenly was capped by the beginnings of a colossal explosion. The screen went white, and then dead, and so did the sound.

"Whew," said Weinbaum. "I wonder what they will be planning to get them off *with*? And just what, by the way, is an alternate-solar planet, and a Fortean tunnel?"

"I never heard of either," Wald said.

"Well, evidently the tunnel is something we're going to discover in the very near future. The ship model shown is contemporary with us, and solid-fuel grains don't have a very long shelf-life. Besides, we can't have been using the Dirac very long by then— as you probably noticed, the reporter committed an elementary failure in technique."

"What was it?" Dana said.

"He forgot to mention the date. We'll have to put out a directive about that. Another spin, please, Thor."

Now the screen showed a flat-on photograph of a spiral galaxy. That it was the Milky Way was made plain by the presence of two satellite galaxies which were obviously the Magellanic Clouds. Given the inclusion of these in the picture, plus the unusually large size of the home lens, Weinbaum quickly estimated that the distance of the camera from the subject could not have been under ten million light years.

The photograph had been turned into a map by the addition of a three-color overlay in red, green, and gray. The red covered a large, irregular area on the southern side of the disc, including the Clouds, while the green covered much more of the northern side. The gray area wandered narrowly between them, but spread out, fan-like, to the west; and there were small patches of gray isolated in both the tinted areas, although most of these were on the red side. Some areas were also cross-hatched. One sun far out on a spiral arm in the red area, near the Clouds, had been marked with a tiny flag, while another deep in the green area seemed to be capped by a sort of tiara.

On the audio, a vibrant lecturer's voice, obviously that of a professional actor, was saying, "The Green Exarchy is generally known to be older than man, but nobody knows man's age. Time is relative; and what with the distortions of interstellar travel, the welter of galactic languages, the different stages of history to be found on every world, the bad communications, and the indifference fostered by longevity, no one can say with confidence even what today's date might be, no, not within a year."

And so much for the directive, Weinbaum thought.

"We may guess, however, that man discovered the Imaginary Drive about four thousand years ago, and emerged from UrSpace to find the Exarchy, or its parent empires, already established. The Exarchy today consists exclusively of non-human races and is still one of the two major centers of power in the galaxy. It is thought to be a tyranny, but the applicability of so anthropocentric a word to a non-human political system is dubious; indeed, we cannot even be sure that the Exarchy is a 'political' system, except as viewed externally.

"The second major power is the loose and shifting confederation of planets dominated by High Earth. These are predominately human or humanoid in population." At the words "High Earth," the flag expanded slightly, just enough to show that it bore some unreadable device, and then shrank to its former size.

"Both systems constantly contend for the independent planets. Of these there are two types. Those populated mainly or entirely by humans are ex-colonies that broke free of High Earth in the past, or were forgotten; these may also bear enclaves of humanoid or non-human aborigines. Those populated mainly by humanoid or non-human peoples are products of independent evolution; a few also tolerate human enclaves.

"The independent planets are almost invariably divided into nation-states. Once such a planet develops a world government, if it does, it tends to gravitate, or be forced, into one of the main power systems.

"Incessant intrigue is therefore the social norm alike upon the independent planets and upon those dominated by High Earth, and has quasi-official status through the Traitors' Guild, an institution now perhaps a thousand years old (or so it claims)."

Here the flag expanded once more until it completely covered the screen. The device upon it could now be seen to be a colorless coat-of-arms. Its crest consisted of a two-faced space helmet, backed by wings, one a bird's, the other a bat's, and wreathed; from the wreath arose a hand flourishing a two-edged sword. The shield was divided down the middle, and showed a coat, one half of which was upside down. The motto read: *Mundus vult decipi.*

"Little is known, necessarily, of the policy of the Guild. Operationally, it has not been above selling an occasional planet to the Green Exarch, but seems firmly to oppose anyone else's doing so. Its methods are deliberately enshrouded in rumor, but in general, seem to place a very high value on solidarity, expertise, and tradition.

"If a social norm prevails under the Exarch, other than the will or policy of the Exarch itself, no official knowledge of it exists in the Confederation."

The screen went dark. Dana Lje said:

"Now *there's* a sticky-sounding situation. if you please. I wonder how many thousands of years it will take for that to evolve? That announcer guessed he was speaking about four thousand years *after* it had begun to jell—but how long from the present will that be?"

"I suspect it will begin sooner than I like to think," Weinbaum said. "We don't have that so-called Imaginary Drive yet—unless that's what they come to call the Haertel Overdrive, for which it doesn't seem to be a very appropriate term—but all the same, we have already made first contact with the Exarchy, as I mentioned briefly to Thor back while we were still searching for you. And I also have a sneaking suspicion that the first seeds of that Traitors' Guild are right here in the bureau, if not in fact in this very room. What does the motto mean, Thor?"

"'The world wishes to be deceived.'"

"Well, so it does," Weinbaum said. "Or maybe that's only a bias forced on me by my line of work. But I remember a quotation from somewhere: 'To conceal from a man his own nature is the easiest of all tasks, and the basis of civilized intercourse.' Machiavelli? Lord

Gro? This is all getting to be pretty heady stuff, isn't it? Spin her again!"

There was no picture with the next transmission, and the voice spoke in Machine, a language probably unknown to Dana Lje, but perfectly intelligible to both Weinbaum and Thor Wald. It said evenly and rapidly, "This is Antarctic Base Two of Central Computation." There was a pause, and then a little pip of pure sound. "We have a case here which may be of some use against the Bird King, but it is also potentially dangerous and presents several anomalies. What appeared at first to be a perfectly ordinary Rebirth Four tribesman named Tlan yesterday stumbled into one of our outposts. He claimed also to harbor the personality of Qvant, the supreme autarch of Rebirth Three, who at last reports was imprisoned in a brain-case in the Rebirth Three Museum, where he was being consulted as a god by Tlan's people and others like them.

"Deep analysis supports the claim, as of course, more trivially, does the distance traveled through Bird country. But the circumstances of Qvant's escape are clouded; moreover, the analysis found distinct traces of previous occupancy by a third personality, dating the year of its origin to '1955.' This style of dating antecedes Rebirth One and thus cannot be any less than twenty-five thousand years in the past.

"Sub-query." *Pip!* "How could time-projection have been known that long ago without significantly changing history—let alone without our having been aware of it?

"Main query." *Pip!* "If this personality was ousted by Qvant, or by Qvant and his host acting in concert, under what circumstances might it have survived beyond the usual two or three seconds in our continuum?"

Weinbaum waited breathlessly for the reply, but there was nothing further.

"Boy, I'd love to hear the answer to that one," he said. "But for all we know, the computer replied on another channel, or just gave them a print-out. I suppose sorting all this material is going to be a major headache in itself."

"Since we cannot know the background situation, the answer to the main query would be of no use to us anyhow," Wald said. "I would have been much more interested in the answer to the sub-query. Miss Lje assumed from what she found in the beep that the future is fixed in every essential respect, though you'll recall that she implied some leeway for small variations 'before a situation goes to completion,' I think she said. Yet roughly twenty-five thousand years from now, they do *not* believe this. I begin to feel that we should make it our first order of business to find out why they disbelieve it."

"Twenty-five thousand years!" Dana Lje said. "Then how on Earth could you understand them?"

"They were addressing a computer in a mathematical language that's universal even now," Weinbaum said. "Mathematics grows with time, but it doesn't change, especially in standard situations like that. Still, Thor, there were enough novelties in that transmission so that we might have misunderstood the implication you suggest."

"If we both heard it the same way, the implication was there. And it is a matter of the highest gravity."

"It can wait," Weinbaum said. "Spin her again."

He was already feeling more than a little dizzy, and had given up taking notes quite a while back. That could come later, all that could come later. Now he wanted only scenes and voices, more and more scenes and voices from the future. They were better than aquavit, even with a beer chaser.

"No. I insist that we consider it now. We stand at the beginning of something in history, the effects of which are absolutely unknown to us. We can be sure only that they will be enormous. If the future is fixed and there is really no such thing as cause-and-effect, as Miss Lje assumes, then it will not matter what we do. If it is not fixed, however, then what we do today in this room may alter the whole fate of mankind, and for all we know, the universe itself. Think, Robin!"

"All right, I guess I'm willing," Weinbaum said with a sigh. "It's time for a break for the potty, anyhow."

CHAPTER TEN: *Weinbaum on Sinai*

"Now," Weinbaum said. "I really don't see how you can expect to solve a problem of that magnitude in what little remains of one afternoon."

"We have just been given a huge hint," Wald said. "If a technologically sophisticated people of twenty-five thousand years from now believes that the future is not fixed, it is plain on the face of it that they know something about the matter that we don't know. Whatever it may be, I take their consequent assumption as a given for the problem. And as I told Miss Lje, the sort of deterministic universe that she pictures was a commonplace of the old relativity theories, so a vast amount of my thinking has already been done for me by better minds than mine, from Galileo to Haertel.

"The idea behind it is that if time is a linear dimension, just like length, height, and width, then the entity that I see before me as Captain Robin Weinbaum is only a second-by-second section through a much larger entity, one of whose extensions is invisible to me. By the way, I wonder if you have any idea how big that entity would be, physically, in four dimensions? Assuming, to keep the figures simple, that Robin lives to be a century old, he would then be roughly a foot thick, two feet wide, five feet five inches in height, and five hundred and eighty-six trillion, five hundred and sixty-nine billion, six hundred million miles in duration. Consider, Miss Lje, the sheer mass of the object you're marrying!

"And the consciousness of Robin Weinbaum is moving

along that entity in that invisible direction. He is not free in any way to change the shaping of the ultimate creature; all he can do is observe, as you noted.

"Now, let me point out that to this day nobody *knows* whether time 'really' is a linear dimension or not. The idea was widely adopted because it greatly simplified mathematics in certain important fields. In the broadest possible terms, what is mechanics in three dimensions becomes statics in four. But a fifth promptly becomes philosophically necessary to contain this system; we find that we actually need a minimum of eight to describe certain processes that go on in atomic nuclei if we resort to quantum mechanics; and although Haertel scrapped all that nonsense, the fact remains that mathematically we are allowed to use any number of dimensions that we find we require for the simplification of any given problem. We often resort to something called Hilbert space, which is described as n-dimensional—it's like modern sex, any number may be played with.

"The point I am getting to is that although statitics may be mathematically more convenient for us than mechanics, this fact may reflect nothing in the real universe except ordinary human laziness. Or, to put the best possible face on the matter, a facet of aesthetics. That's really all the law of parsimony comes down to, you know, Robin: we *prefer* the simplest theory that fits all the facts, but nobody has ever been able to prove that it is a real law of nature."

"Objection," Weinbaum said. "Dana, do you know what a world-line is?"

"No, it's just a word I heard in the beep."

"I guessed as much. It happens to be one of those relativistic entities Thor is talking about: The total history of an object, as viewed in all four dimensions, like that umpty-trillion-mile-long pink worm you're marrying. You overheard a cruiser traveling along such a world-line; you couldn't have made up such an odd term; and the fact that somebody in the future can cruise a world-line would seem to me to establish that world-lines really exist."

"Granted," Thor Wald said instantly. "But, Robin, I never said that they couldn't, or didn't. There's a difference between a convenience and a fiction. What is further establish by this datum is that if somebody can travel a world-line—and you may remember that that cruiser was actually going *backward* in time—then this implies not only the convenience but the actual reality of a *five*-dimensional frame, at a minimum."

"But . . ." The girl put a hand helplessly to her forehead. "I don't understand what that means at all. And even if I did, I wouldn't be able to understand how anything we did could have any effect upon it. If we can't change things in the fourth dimension, if we can't even see in that direction, what good does the existence of a fifth do us?"

"We can see in that direction a little now, thanks to you," Thor Wald said. "And as for what it means, well, it means that the universe of mechanics is restored; and, in some metamathematical sense which it is now imperative for us to work out, so is free will."

"In more practical terms," Weinbaum said somberly, "it means that you have placed an intolerable burden on us, Dana. It means that these events in the beep are only potentially real; and that we, as mere mortal men, have been given the power to select which of them we wish to have happen, for unknowable thousands of centuries to come. We may look at the quincunx of time from above, and decide now which tree we wish to cut down, and which we will let live. And we do not have the wisdom. We have the power—but not the wisdom."

"We shall have to learn it," Thor Wald said.

Weinbaum stared straight ahead. Suddenly, everyone and everything in the room was strange to him. He felt as though he had been enclosed in a glacier for 25,000 years.

"No," he said. "We three are not gods. We are a reporter, a physicist, and a security officer. No exercise of will can make any of us other than what we are, or more thean marginally better than who we are. To think even for an instant that we shall ever have the wisdom to handle this insane gift is in itself madness of the highest order. The Greeks had a name for that madness: *hubris*, or overweening pride. And they left us cautionary tales about it in great plenty."

"Do you think, then, that muddling through would be any better?" Thor Wald said. "History has left us a few cautionary tales about that, too, Robin."

"Of course not."

"Then what," Dana Lje said, "do you propose to do? How can you both choose, and not choose?"

"I propose to enforce modesty upon our successors. It is the only exercise of this power that I would dare to permit myself, now or ever again. By the time we three leave this room, I hope it will be permanently impossible for *any* human being to believe either that he has, or can ever learn, the wisdom to train and prune the jungle of the future into a formal garden or monkey-puzzle. I may not succeed, but I am going to try."

"On what principle?" Thor Wald said.

"Why, upon the only principle we have ever encountered which permits a man to both choose, and not choose," Weinbaum said. "I may be addressing it to nothing but a sort of cosmic Dead Letter Office, but that can't be helped. The message itself is plain. It has got to read:

"To Whom it may concern: Thy will, not mine."

AN EPILOGUE: *Which Asserts Nothing*

The indoctrination tape ended, and Krasna touched a button. The holograph tank darkened, and folded silently back into the desk. The office lights came back up.

"They didn't see their way through to us, not by a long shot, but they didn't need to," he said. "They took the general steps, and left the details as free to take care of themselves as they possibly could. They didn't see, for instance, that when one section of the government becomes nearly all-knowing—no matter how small it was to begin with—it necessarily becomes all of the government that there is. Thus the bureau turned into the Service, and pushed everyone else out. The Traitors' Guild is yet to come, and we don't worry about it yet.

"On the other hand, those people did come to be afraid that a government with an all-knowing arm might become a rigid dictatorship. That couldn't happen, and didn't happen, because the more you know, the wider your field of possible operations becomes, and the more fluid and dynamic a society you need. How could a rigid society expand to other star systems, let alone other galaxies? It couldn't be done."

"I should think it could," Jo said slowly. "After all, if you know in advance what everybody is going to do—"

"But we don't, Jo. That's just a popular fiction—or, if you like, a red herring. Not all the business of the cosmos is carried on over the Dirac, after all. The only events we can ever overhear are those which are transmitted as a message. Do you order your lunch over the Dirac? Of course you don't. Up to now, you've never said a word over the Dirac in your life. Nor would it be possible for us to mount moment-by-moment surveillance over the billions of sentient creatures scattered through space-time, even if we had an instrument suitable for it. We don't even know how many of them there are.

"And there's much more to it than that. All dictatorships are based on the proposition that government can somehow control a man's thoughts. From the four-dimensional point of view which we provisionally adopt— and please note well that 'provisionally'—we know that the consciousness of the observer is the only free thing in the universe. Wouldn't we look foolish trying to control that, when our working physics shows that it's impossible to do so? That's why the Service is in no sense a thought police. We're interested only in acts. We're an Event Police."

"But why?" Jo said. "If all history is fixed, why do we bother with these boy-meets-girl assignments, for instance? The meetings will happen anyhow."

"They will and they won't," Krasna said. "I see you haven't yet deduced the actual nature of Weinbaum's decision. So let's continue to look at it for a while from the point of view of Dana Lje's deterministic universe, which ninety percent of the time is the way we do look at it. Our interests as a government depend upon the future. We operate as if the future is as real as the past, and so far we haven't been disappointed: the Service is entirely successful. But even within this frame, that very success isn't without its warnings. What would happen if we *stopped* supervising events?

"We no more know now than we did in Thor Wald's day whether the universe is truly deterministic or not;

and in fact, the metamathematics that he later developed to handle the question showed quite convincingly that we'd have no more chance of understanding the answer if we got it than a leaf understands the photosynthesis that's going on inside it."

"How could anybody *prove* such a thing?"

"Well ... I don't know whether you've ever heard of anybody named Gödel, but he was child's play compared to Wald, so I'm not going to attempt to explain the demonstration. You can study it later, if you feel up to it. Let me put it in a more general way. In the history of science, you encounter things called paradigms—defined by Kuhn as 'universally recognized scientific achievements that for a time provide model problems and solutions to a community of practitioners.' These preconceptions govern how we look at the universe, and therefore what we see in it. The Ptolemaic system, Copernicanism, Galilean relativity, the electromagnetic theory, Einsteinean relativity, Haertelism, these are all obvious examples.

"Scientists find it difficult to break out of the *current* paradigm. The informed layman, and even more the man on the street, is usually stuck in the *previous* one. Thus in Einstein's lifetime, there was a widespread belief that his ideas were just fanciful foolishness and that it was Newton who really had had the straight goods. In an age when Haertel's was the going paradigm, Miss Lje was still seeing *her* universe from the point of view of General Relativity—Einstein's. And for scientists themselves, they tend to stick to the current one until the evidence for its successor becomes absolutely overwhelming.

"Now in the beep, we are confronted with vast masses of evidence that don't fit into the current paradigm.

What is much, much worse is that we are confronted with many *future* paradigms, which not only conflict with ours but with each other. Wald's metalanguage simply shows that the very structure of science itself makes it impossible for us to choose among them, because that structure is in itself one of those paradigms. Follow?"

"Well, at a distance, but I may never catch up," Jo said frankly.

"I think you will. Anyhow, though we have a vast mass of evidence that the future is fixed, every single piece of that evidence is superficial. As a result, we have to take on the role of the caretaker of inevitability. We believe that nothing can possibly go wrong ... but we have to act on the philosophy that history helps only those who help themselves.

"That's why we safeguard huge numbers of courtships right through to contract, and even beyond it—we have even revived the Italian Renaissance custom of legal witnesses to consummation. We have to see to it that *every single person who is mentioned in any Dirac 'cast gets born*. Our obligation as Event Police is to make the events of the future possible, because those events are crucial to the evolution of our society—even the smallest of them. That is simply one single example of Weinbaum's general decision. Can you figure out now what that was?"

"I think so," Jo said, very slowly indeed. "He decided that *everything had to happen*. Everything, good or bad."

Krasna nodded approvingly. "Absolutely correct. The only way to safeguard the future from the Dirac transmitter in the hands of some mad-man who thinks he's a god is to make no selection whatsoever. If an event is mentioned in the Dirac beep, then by God we rush there and *make* it happen—whether we like it or not. The very fact that we increasingly like the results indicates